RIVULET OF DARKNESS

BOOK II
The Disembodied Voice

ALBERT B. GARCIA

Published by EDK Books and
Distributed by EDK Distribution, LLC
edkbooksanddistribution.com
edkbooksanddistribution@gmail.com | (206) 227-8179

ISBN: 978-1-956065-17-6

Library of Congress Control Number: 2022913485

Printed in the United States of America

Editor: Barbara Kindness
Cover Design-Book Layout: Julie K. Lee @ Lee Creative

TABLE OF CONTENTS

CHAPTER I

RESURFACE

THE WORLD PLACED UPON ME has become an empty hole filled with the darkness consuming every part of who I am. Inside this mysterious darkness I proclaim to be an empty world, I am being pulled into an unknown profane path filled with all its negative energy along with all the things hidden deep within, only to appear inside my nightmares.

Having never experienced the terrifying images before, I now have these dark figures appearing before me but undisclosed to the world that I must live in. Yet, their presence has continued to torment me without any reason. Only leaving an unpleasant stench that lingers when the night sets in along with the silence that draws in all the dark energy that lurks inside this *unknown darkness*.

Often, I feel myself becoming disembodied as I become weightless. I open my eyes and feel my body lifted into the air. Panic starts to set in as I look up toward the ceiling. I cannot move my body . . . so scared from not having any control of what is happening. I continue to panic while feeling myself levitating above my bed. My body starts to spin around the room in slow motion. I am so terrified. I try to lift my head to look around. I start to gasp as the walls circle right past me, faster and faster. *Please GOD . . . make this stop!* I feel so scared of what could be inside this bedroom with me. At that moment, all I can think about is the possibility of something dark trying to overtake me. Suddenly, the nightmare ends with me falling from high above the air and landing back onto my bed with a sinking feeling inside my stomach. I cannot help but wonder if the nightmares were from an experience I had from the past. In the back of my mind, I believe something dark has returned to terrorize me during the night when I am sound asleep. There is an unsettling possibility that the evil entity that once moved around our house during the night . . . never left.

Unfortunately, those forgotten memories have now resurfaced. I am reliving those familiar emotions I once faced when I stood by and watched the most important person disappear into the darkness. Having felt this tragic "loss," the sadness still lingers while the pain never seems to go away. A "loss," forcing me to face the memories of a devastating time planted inside my mind. Those same memories that leave behind the "whispers" I hear when I find myself waking up inside a cold, dark room from sleepwalking. The same whispers that assure me that my brother David is still here with me, even after his death.

I can hear the words so clearly as if my brother was standing near me, whispering those same words I first heard two years ago when I stood behind the bathroom door after watching David's soul disappear into the darkness. I can still hear him say, *"I was living with the fear that was coming from within myself when, in fact, the experiences I was going through were all the memories of what happened to me. So scared of what I saw, of what I thought to be just a part of what I was going through only to find out that I was an illusion of my own existence . . . "*

Along with his whispers, the memory of my brother David will live on through me. But something else has returned. I believe the evil presence that once appeared during the night along with David's spirit has been hiding inside the darkness, just waiting to find its way back to finish what it started with him. I believe that I will have to face what my brother had once feared, and somehow find a way to make this Dark Entity disappear.

. . . .

It is the winter of 1983. The rain, along with the wind, is coming through my bedroom window. The window is difficult to close because the wood frame that holds the glass has become warped from all the years of earlier storms that have come through. Lifting the old, stained curtain to look outside into the dark, I am unable to see anything with the dark clouds blocking out the moonlight. I can smell the damp air from the rain coming in as the winter brings back the memory of the night my family and I saw the soul and the spirit of my brother finally laid to rest. It has been about two years since I stood by the bathroom door and felt my brother David disappear into the night as my Aunt Vera helped my parents through this tough time.

Aunt Vera, who practiced White Magic, saw this dark figure of a little boy inside her motor home when her family stopped by to visit for a couple of days while parked in our backyard late at night. She felt a connection with the little boy that appeared in the hallway of their motor home. As the small, dark figure disappeared into the darkness, she soon knew who he was. Aunt Vera found herself facing a tough time trying to tell my parents about everything she experienced in her motor home. However, after leaving our house, Aunt Vera felt she needed to tell my parents. Knowing what she found out, she let them know that she would be coming over to tell them something important in person.

When she arrived, she explained that the spirit in her motor home was David and he needed help to be at peace. Soon after, Aunt Vera would also find herself facing the evil entity that had attached itself to my father only to terrorize David's soul. Eventually, she would confront the spirit of the little boy that turned out to be David, who was watching over his own soul as the evil presence was trying to take him. The Dark Entity that attached itself to my father when he confronted this *evil* had forced us to relive the tragedy of David's death on that cold, dark night close to three in the morning.

I am still unsure of what I experienced that night, but I knew everything that my father had told my mother and my Aunt Vera had explained what was going on inside our house. That tragic night everything took a turn. The experience was overwhelming as I watched in horror this Dark Entity trying to take control of David's soul. David was unaware of its plan to drag him back into its world. At that moment, I felt the presence of something evil along with David's soul as he found himself staring directly at this Dark Entity. I could sense David's fear facing this thing that terrorized him while unaware of his own existence trapped between two worlds.

· · · · · · ·

Unfortunately, now, two years later, after Aunt Vera helped David's spirit come together with its soul to find peace, I have started to face again the nightmares and the vivid images I once experienced when David's soul was here with me. But now, something more is happening. Dark figures have now started to appear during the night.

I decided to move into the back bedroom where I had once sensed my brother's soul was here with me. When I would wake up from sleepwalking, I would find myself standing in the dark. Even though I felt the presence of David's soul inside this bedroom, I felt more sadness from missing my brother than the fear of seeing his spirit appear to me.

Regardless of the nightmares, something is wrong and everything that I had experienced two years ago has returned. Only this time, I fear that whatever it is has come back for *me*. I believe something bad is about to happen and without the presence of David's soul inside this house I will have to face this alone. Unfortunately, what is happening now I cannot tell my parents about anything that is going on with me. I cannot watch my mother relive those painful memories of losing her son all over again. Somehow, I need to find a way to end this nightmare—this nightmare that has caused something terrible to resurface and haunt this house once again.

Without having the presence of David's spirit or soul here with me to connect with the *Supernatural World,* I will have to face this experience alone and not knowing what lies ahead. One thing for sure—there is a possibility that what my brother went through could very well put me in the same situation that ended his life. I fear the evil presence has come back. The Dark Entity once hidden inside this back bedroom that I now occupy will come back for me as it once did for my brother's soul. Stopped by my Aunt Vera, her practice of White Magic never allowed the Entity to succeed in dragging David's soul into its world, only leaving behind the stench of its evil presence.

Although time has gone by, the fears that once connected the world that I live in and the world that I saw through my brother's eyes have faded, leaving behind the scars that project through the emotions that stay hidden deep inside my thoughts. The revenant of this dark evil energy has become an old moldy stench that seems to linger inside the darkness that continues to stay with me and my parents, making it difficult to forget about the tragedy that has changed our lives.

The pain, along with my fears, has grown into an *Imaginary Carousel* that never stops turning. It seems as if something bad is holding me back from living my life. A surreal force seems to feed off the pain I keep inside, and the fears I face each night from the nightmares that never seem to go away. My abiding fear is that this force, feeding off my emotions, is coming from the dark figures watching me sleep during the night, and is causing these disembodied nightmares while devouring every part of who I am; that is, *My Soul.*

I am facing the same fear that David once did. The fear that something dark has attached itself deep inside my soul, forcing me to face the same Dark Entities he saw himself up against. I once sensed my brother's soul slowly suffering while drawn into a mysterious world by an evil entity that followed my father home from Aunt Barbara's house. It attached itself to my father, almost dragging David's soul into its world of endless suffering.

It has been two years since David's soul found peace. I can only hope that God gives me the strength to defeat this dark energy that has resurfaced from the past. I am facing something evil channeling all its dark energy into my nightmares—the nightmares that haunt me each night, manifesting these pitch-black images of dark figures standing around my bed when I am asleep. The same images that watch me during the night when I am standing alone inside the back bedroom unaware of how I got there. Unlike before, when my parents and I first moved into this house, I would find myself standing inside the back bedroom only sensing David's spirit with me.

Now something strange has started to occur. I needed to move into this bedroom to find out what is now happening after David's spirit left us two years ago. I feel as if I am facing the same evil that haunted my brother, but I believe that this dark energy has followed us for a while. Something is using our fear along with the pain that my parents and I have carried, like a curse placed upon this family. I only hope that everything that my family and I have gone through will stay hidden in the back of our minds. So then, I could live the life that I had always hoped for without facing the fears that my brother suffered during the brief time he was alive with us.

CHAPTER 2

THE TRAGEDY

I . . . ROBERT DE LE CRUZ could never forget that my brother David De Le Cruz, two years older than I, would suffer the fate from another family member's selfish and reckless behavior, never having a chance to grow up to become an adult.

The remnant of David's legacy would end, and the memory of his existence would be hindered by a tragic incident that continues to follow me today.

My life growing up with David was difficult at times. Like any other relationship between two brothers growing up in the 1970s, we were always trying to find ways to get what the other one had. Such as comic books, marbles, or just about anything given to us by our parents. I was close to David as we were growing up with a father who had a drinking problem and a tough time holding onto a job. My brother and I would hide in the closet when our father would come home drunk from a bar. He would force my mother to give him more money to continue drinking while yelling for me and my brother to bring our asses over to him; screaming at us for no reason.

David and I were too scared to go around our dad so we would hide quietly in the closet until he got money from Mom to leave for another couple of days. He would go over to his family's house to drink until it was time for him to return home to get ready for another long week of work. He didn't do this often, but it did not take a whole lot for him to have his first drink and forget about everything that was important to him, including holding on to a job. He would be too sick to go back to work from having too much to drink over the weekend. When he would find himself without a job, we would have to struggle until he found work, not realizing that we would be too weak to go to school from not having anything to eat. Eventually, David and I found ourselves moving out of our house into another house because of falling behind on the rent.

We still enjoyed happy moments together as a family when we would take trips to the mountains in Pop's brown 1972 Ford Galaxy. Our trip seemed so exciting, especially when Pop would pull over to stop on the side of the road to eat the sandwiches Mom made with the bologna and cheese she brought from home. I would look at my brother and see how happy he looked. David would stare out the car window smiling and pointing at everything around him while eating his sandwich.

Our parents would allow us to get out of the car to look around. Mom made sure David and I stayed close by so she could keep an eye on us. She always had this concerned look when telling us not to wander off too far, worried about our getting lost or hurt. I would follow my brother as he picked up rocks and sticks to throw into the trees. Everything around us felt so peaceful as the birds moved throughout the trees and the buzzing sounds from the insects seemed to be coming from everywhere. I could hear the branches breaking with every step we took then becoming startled by our parents' voices echoing all around us to come back to the car.

At that moment, I thought about how boring life would be without having my older brother around. The trips we had with our parents allowed us to forget about all the sad things we had to face at home. Like finding ourselves moving out once again from the house that my parents had just rented. Having to move from one house to another because of our father's drinking problem, placing so much anxiety on me and my brother. Having to make new friends from moving so much would only lead up to being bullied by the other kids. Having to cope with this burden, David and I became very protective of each other, making sure that we kept each other safe from anyone wanting to harm us.

Often those difficult moments would disappear for a brief time when our parents would once again find the time to drive us to the mountains or coast with the little money we had. Spending most of our time on a long trip listening to Pop's stories about when he was young made me feel as if I already knew his whole family, even though our parents never took us to go visit any of them while we were growing up.

I never thought about how difficult our dad made our lives with the other stranger who lived inside him. I never thought about the other person he would become when he would appear to us as this mean stranger coming into our house to terrorize us; as if he had one body with two people living inside when he would start drinking. I feared the man that would visit us after he would take his first drink of alcohol. I watched this stranger slowly emerge from the darkness that came from deep within our dad to enter our lives. I would see this selfish, mean, and uncaring stranger who scared me and my brother into hiding when he came looking for us. Only in that moment did I realize we did not have our father to protect us. Just the hope for this other man to go away and give us back our father.

Nevertheless, my mother always made sure when the strange man came over to visit, she would send us to our bedroom to keep us safe from this terrible man we feared so much. Mom would explain to us that Pop was really a good person who every now and then would let the mean man come out when he started to drink his alcohol. Our mother would never say anything bad about him to us, even though he was mean to her. Regardless of how he treated her when he became drunk, my mother always tried her best to keep us away from him as he would become more belligerent when she refused to give in to what he wanted, like the money that our mom did not have.

As time went by, David started to become distant and withdrawn from us and I felt something strange was happening to him. I did not understand what was going on other than what my brother and I had to face trying to adjust to the life we were living. David would sit on his bed listening to music on his clock radio that sat on a small table near him, not wanting to talk to anyone. Other times, he would just sit on his bed drawing these dark figures on a piece of lined paper and then place the pictures in a hole in the wall of our closet. I would ask him about his pictures, and he would tell me about these dark figures appearing inside the nightmares he was experiencing.

Strange things started to happen to David. I would look at him as he stared at his drawing of a dark figure he had sketched and a dazed look came across his face. As if something was making him act different. I would ask David to go outside with me to play and he would refuse to leave our bedroom. Our parents did not notice David acting strangely, but I knew something was wrong with him. I knew he would have gotten mad at me if I told our mother about the way he was acting.

Then he started to get worse; to become distant from my parents, refusing to leave his bedroom, not wanting to sit at the kitchen table to eat with us as a family. David would get up from his bed and wake me up in the middle of the night saying that he would hear a knocking coming across the wall behind him. I was not sure what he was talking about because I never heard any noises when I slept through the night. I did not think anything about what he said since we shared the same bedroom. I would have heard the knocking going across the wall, since my bed was close to his bed.

We lived in a small one-bedroom house in town, so David and I had to share our bedroom with my parents. My parents' bed was across from our bed on the other side of the room. David always slept with his head near the wall that faced the backyard. My bed was along the wall that separated the living room and our bedroom. My head always faced the entrance of the doorway going into the living room, making it difficult for me to go to sleep when our parents would watch television late at night.

I would wake up in the middle of the night listening for any knocking coming from where David was sleeping. I did not hear any noises like David described; only the panic in David's voice when he would talk in his sleep as if he was being chased by something terrifying. I would go over and sit quietly on his bed. The next day I would ask him about the nightmares from the night before. He would ignore me and continue to draw a dark figure on a piece of paper. Watching David continue to act so strangely, I wondered if I needed to tell our parents after all.

Being so young and feeling as if David were pushing me away, I really did not know what was going on as I tried to forget about his strange pictures and the nightmares he would experience during the night. I only wanted to spend time with my brother since we only had each other. I continued waiting for David to get better so we could do all the things we used to do Unfortunately, things got worse. Then something horrific happened—something that every parent should never have to experience.

David got sick with a fever and started to hallucinate. My mother put him to bed, giving him medicine to help him sleep. Later that night, David woke me up. He called me over to his bed to tell me about the knocking going across his wall. In a whispering voice, he told me it sounded as if the noise was coming from outside the house just above where he lay his head down to sleep. I stood by his bed, and I could see how pale he looked with sweat covering his face. He whispered to me, "I can see a dark figure at the foot of my bed watching me."

I began to get scared, looking around our room. I could not see what David was looking at.

I told him, "Mom wants you to get some rest so you can feel better in the morning."

I walked back to my bed, feeling so cold while smelling the dampness of the rain coming through the bedroom windows as the air pushed its way in from outside. I could hear David talking as if he were talking to someone next to him. I finally went to bed, still hearing the wind pushing up against our house along with the cracking sounds coming from the walls. I heard our parents getting ready for bed. Pop switched off all the lights throughout the house while Mom gave David his medicine to help him sleep.

Just as I closed my eyes, I heard a smashing sound along with our front door slamming against the wall. I quickly covered my head with my blanket and felt someone walk near me as they entered our bedroom. Now I was so frightened and wide awake. I heard a man's voice telling my father to get out of bed, simultaneously hearing David moaning and whispering in his sleep, having one of his nightmares.

Lowering my blanket to see what was happening, I could hear Pop telling this other person to go home and sleep it off. I could not see anything other than a dark figure standing near my parents' bed. I was not sure who it was, only hearing another man's voice sounding terribly angry. I could hear the other man saying he had a gun pointed at his head. At that moment, I began to get *really* scared as I stared toward the shadow of a man now standing over my father. Suddenly, I heard this man say, *"I had cursed one of your kids to die in seven years . . . "*

I was scared and did not understand what was going on, still hearing our dad trying to convince this strange man to go home because he had had too much to drink. Soon, I heard their voices become louder. Sitting up in bed, I began to see a struggle between Pop and this strange man, suddenly hearing a loud bang echoing across the bedroom. Quickly looking over to where David was sleeping, I saw Mom running over to his bed while looking directly at me with a frightening look on her face. Slowly, I got out of bed and walked over to where she was holding David in her arms. She cried loudly while moving the hair over to the side of his forehead with her fingers. She was calling David's name to wake up, but David just lay in her arms with his eyes closed. I stood at the foot of my brother's bed and watched my mother cry with so much pain coming from her voice. I did not really know what was going on around me.

I looked over to where I heard our dad yelling at this man he called Eddie. He kept yelling, "Why would you do this to us . . . why?"

I watched this man pacing back and forth along the floor, holding something in his hand, tapping repeatedly against the wall. He kept wailing while saying how sorry he was, over and over. Pop quickly walked over to me and told me to leave the room. I walked out of the bedroom over to the couch in the living room to sit down. Suddenly I looked up and heard people coming in through the front entrance where Eddie had forced his way in by kicking open the door. I could see police officers rushing into our house and going into our bedroom. I continued to sit on the couch unaware of what was happening while trying to listen to what was going on. Suddenly, I saw these people walk through the front door into the bedroom with a stretcher.

After sitting on the couch impatiently waiting for a while, I watched these people come out of the bedroom while taking David away on a stretcher. As David went by, he looked directly at me with tears running down the sides of his face. He looked as if he was trying to say something. I ran up to him and, leaning on the side of the stretcher, was trying to hear what he was saying. Walking beside David, I heard him whisper, "I saw the dark figure . . . "

The people carrying David on the stretcher suddenly stopped me from going any farther. I just stood there watching David being lifted into the back of the ambulance. I started to cry for my brother even though I did not know what was happening to him. As the ambulance started to drive away, I saw my parents come out of the house. Our father's arms were tightly wrapped around my mother while her cries became very loud, echoing throughout the night as she called out for David. I continued to watch as Pop tried to pick up Mom from the ground after she fell to her knees watching David taken away.

I walked back into the house still feeling shaken while wiping the tears from my eyes with the back of my hands. I walked toward our bedroom, stopping just outside the door as I was trying to see what the police were doing to this man. I could see police officers standing around him as he sat on the floor with his back against the wall, crying with both hands over his face. They finally picked him up from the floor, handcuffing him and placing him under arrest. I watched this strange man walk right past me and say, "I'm so sorry, Robert. I'm so sorry . . ."

I stared at this person and wondered how he knew my name, although my only concern right then was trying to find out about my brother. Walking back into the house, my father helped my mother over to the couch as she continued to cry, and I still was not understanding what had just occurred. I walked over to Pop and asked him in a low, whispering voice, "Who is that man?"

He quietly answered, "He is your Uncle Eddie, my older brother."

I looked at my father, unable to understand why my Uncle Eddie would do something so bad to us. Not saying anything else about Uncle Eddie, I asked about David and when he would be coming back home.

Pop looked at me for a moment with tears coming down his face. "I'm sorry, Robert . . . David won't be coming home . . . he was hurt really bad . . ."

I said, "Did Uncle Eddie hurt him?"

"Yes . . ."

Refusing to believe what Pop had told me about David not coming home, I started to cry. I became angry, asking him why he would not be coming home when he spoke to me before going into the ambulance. I explained to our dad about David seeing a dark figure, even though I was not sure if he was talking about Uncle Eddie or the dark figure from his nightmare. Pop stared at me as if he did not understand what I just told him, because he knew David already had died in Mom's arms as she held him on his bed while wiping the blood off his face.

At that moment, my whole life changed knowing that my brother David would never be coming home. I would have to face the emptiness of living my life without him. Never seeing him smile again when he would grab me by the arm to show me something he found outside, or excited about something given to him and wanting to share it with me.

Soon after the incident, my parents and I moved out of our one-bedroom house in town. We left behind all the memories of that tragic night which changed our lives forever. Unfortunately, moving from that one-bedroom house into our new home in the country would not only be a new beginning, but the start of a dark evil presence entering my world. Whether this dark presence had always been with us or already living in the home, I was unaware of what it was. This would be the beginning of something surreal. I would become confused about what was real or what was just a figment of my imagination, as this dark presence started to make itself known during the night and inside my nightmares. I never thought about the fact that the things I started to experience after leaving the other house were the same things my brother had already gone through. I never understood what was happening to David, only aware that the signs had become a warning of what was going to happen to him.

My brother unknowingly saw signs of his own tragic death. Even though David talked to me about the strange things he was experiencing, I was too young at the time to understand. I never concluded that the signs were a coincidence or a warning unfolding right in front of me. However, the thought of what he experienced stood out in the back of my mind as a prediction or warning that *he* only saw. Like the knocking sound David heard going across his bedroom wall at night. This could have been the same knocking sound I heard when Uncle Eddie was hitting the barrel of the gun against the bedroom wall while pacing up and down along the floor after realizing he had just shot David. Also realizing that the dark figure David drew on a piece of paper from his nightmares could have been the same dark figure of Uncle Eddie standing over our father pointing a gun to his head, leading up to David's death.

Those "signs" appearing to him seemed to be "supernatural" placed inside David by someone or something evil. As if something spiritually dark was keeping track of David, using his own uncle to accidentally kill him "in order" to possess his soul. Nevertheless, something else happened to David's soul during that moment of his death. David never left us. He became trapped between both worlds. The world David left behind and the other world that lies hidden inside the darkness.

Leaving the past behind would become difficult to face as things started to happen once my family and I moved to the house in the country to start a new life. Unfortunately, David's spirit remained with us along with the bad memories we thought were behind in the one-bedroom house in town. This experience with something supernatural was occurring during a grim time for me and my family and would have us relive the pain all over again.

What started to appear was not just signs of David's presence but something else evil hidden inside the darkness coming for my brother's soul. This was a curse brought upon by something evil. Aunt Vera, who knew what my family and I were up against, was the only one capable of stopping it. Aunt Vera sensed the evil presence, unaware of how or why it was in our house. It was not until later when Pop would finally tell the truth of how it could have ended up here with us. Fortunately, Aunt Vera defeated the evil Entity, forcing it back into the darkness and allowing David's spirit to be set free. Finally free from having to never face the Entity haunting me during the night again, I could now have the peace of living a normal childhood.

It's been two years since putting David's soul to rest. Witnessing the night, David's spirit finally left while driving the Entity out of our home. Unfortunately, something else started to happen—the presence of something evil was back. I was not sure if the negative energy had ever left this house as my Aunt Vera used her White Magic to force out its rotted stench from our home. There could also be a good possibility that this Entity was always here with us, just waiting inside the darkness only to resurface and feed off the fear, which strengthened its evil energy, staying hidden like the shadows, masking in the night.

CHAPTER 3

THE APPARITION

I GRADUALLY OPEN MY EYES AND stare into the darkness, thinking about David's spirit that once occupied this empty dark space at the back of the house with a window facing an old barn.

These cold nights seem to trap the unsettling energy surrounding our house. A house sitting alone in the middle of an orchard filled with big "old" walnut trees, which come to life during the darkest hour of the night, like distorted figures dancing to the whistling sounds of the wind. Having scattered thoughts go through my mind at three in the morning, I force myself to go back to sleep even though I am having this uneasy feeling that something bad is about to happen. Even though it's been several months since I changed bedrooms, there are strange things starting to happen during the night when I find myself waking up from having the same nightmare—again and again.

I start off levitating to the ceiling of my bedroom as I become disembodied, suddenly falling back into my body while waking up with a sinking feeling inside my stomach. I feel as if there is a presence coming from inside my bedroom trying to possess me while I sleep. It is difficult to know what is happening when everything around me seems so vague. There are nights I can hear strange noises that seem to come from inside this bedroom. I do not know if it is coming from inside my mind when I am asleep or if something is here with me. I could hear things sliding across my floor or someone walking around my bedroom. Even though I have not been sleepwalking for a while, I am still having a tough time getting up in the morning and catching the bus for school.

I can only force myself to fall back to sleep while ignoring the fact that something dark is here with me and I am unaware of its intentions. Like most nights, after getting two more hours of sleep after waking up from a nightmare, I feel relieved to see the sun coming through the stained curtain covering my window. My bedroom still feels very cold from the long winter we have been having. The lack of having a full night's rest has turned into a struggle between trying to concentrate on what I am doing in class and following directions given to me by my teacher.

Today is Friday. I have an entire day until Christmas vacation starts. I am excited about sleeping in every day for the next two weeks without having to rush around getting ready for school. I can hear my parents in the kitchen while smelling breakfast made. I gradually crawl out of bed knowing my mother will soon be walking into my bedroom to make sure I am getting myself ready for school.

Today, especially important, because it's the last day of school and Christmas is just around the corner. I just could not wait for this day to be over with. I could hear my mother calling me for breakfast while I stood in the mirror splashing water on my head, trying to comb my hair back. I quickly finished what I was doing and walked into the kitchen, watching my mother, a petite lady with black, shoulder-length hair falling onto her face, placing my breakfast on the kitchen table. I sat at the table looking at my mother, unable to tell her about my nightmares, even though she would patiently listen to me.

My mother, Katherine De Le Cruz, is a kind person who would do anything for anyone, especially making sure that my father and I have what we need. She always seems to look so tired, wearing an old yellow apron around her waist to keep food from falling onto her denim skirt. I feel a sense of security when I'm around my mother as she tries to protect me all the time, especially now—since experiencing the loss of David. Regardless of what she has gone through, she still finds the strength to wake up early every morning to make lunch for Pop, along with making sure that I have had my breakfast before leaving the house. Having to start very early, my father, Frank De Le Cruz, leaves for work by six-thirty in the morning to take care of different types of fruit trees and a large walnut orchard on the farm that we live on.

I remember when Pop first looked sad, having to move us into the country closer to his job while living rent free on a ranch, which he would be taking care of for a local farmer who owned half the land in the area. I knew at that moment my father was leaving behind a part of himself in that house, and forever carrying with him the agonizing thought of never having the chance to bring along his oldest son.

As time went by, my father seemed to have changed from being this person who battled his disease of alcoholism to holding in this pain of blaming himself for allowing the incident to escalate to the death of his son. Now, every day, my father comes home and doesn't want to be bothered by anyone as he sits in his chair watching television until he goes to bed. Pop ignores everything around him, until he calls out my name needing something done around the house. I feel as if he does not want anybody to know how he feels by never bringing up David's name. I look on my father, a big, quiet man with a scraggly beard he brushes with his hand, standing five feet ten, who seldom smiles making it difficult for me to talk to him.

Suddenly, upon hearing my mother's voice telling me to go to school, I ran outside feeling the freezing air hit me as the bus approached. I sat in the back, staring out the window toward our house as we drove off. The thought of leaving behind what lies in the house during the day allowed me to forget what I knew I must face each night, giving me a sense of peace for the moment. It made me feel like a normal child to be away from the fear that seemed to be waiting for me when I got back home.

Finally arriving at school, I gradually walked into my classroom and sat down at my desk along the wall, next to a window overlooking a large grass field we used to play soccer on. Miss Mendez calls our names to see who is here with her raspy voice that catches everyone's attention. She stands in front of the class dressed in a long-sleeve shirt and denim jeans. I do not think I've ever seen her wearing anything else other than those flannel shirts she wears with her long braid running down her back.

As Miss Mendez continued going through our names to see who was here, I felt this chill run through me as if something cold just went by. Suddenly, the classroom became quiet with everybody's mouth still moving in slow motion. I started to feel strange as I turned to look out the window ignoring what was happening to me. Continuing to look from one end of the field to the other, I saw a little boy standing at a distance by himself staring back at me. As I tried to remember where I had seen him before, he started to move his mouth as if he were talking to me. I tried to catch my breath, suddenly realizing he was the same little boy in brown corduroy pants I saw two years ago when my Aunt Vera used her spiritual ability to free David's soul from the Dark Entity. Only later did I find out that the spirit of the little boy (the boy in corduroy pants), who had followed David's soul around, were one and the same. Aunt Vera helped bring together David's spirit and soul to find peace and only after she had ridden the Dark Entity from dragging them both into its dark world.

I ran out of my classroom, feeling disoriented and confused as I made my way into the restroom. Quickly pushing open the door to the stall, I started to vomit inside the toilet. After I had bent over the toilet bowl for a while, I walked over to the sink and washed my face. Feeling embarrassed about what happened, I returned to my classroom, noticing everyone staring at me as I walked back to my desk. I was still confused as I sat down looking out the window to find the little boy gone.

Class was finally over. I sat quietly staring out the window with a distant look on my face. I slowly got up from my seat to leave but Miss Mendez stopped me just before I walked out of her classroom. She asked me if everything was okay?

I said, "Yes." Then she said, "I noticed that your eyes had rolled back as you practically stumbled out of the classroom. I followed you to the restroom and was standing outside the door, calling your name. I could hear you mumbling words while vomiting in the toilet. You did not respond, so I walked into the restroom to see if you were okay."

"I don't remember you coming into the restroom, Miss Mendez."

She stared at me with a concerned look on her face, saying, "How could you not remember? You looked up at me with this strange smile and said, *'They are coming for him'* . . . I asked you who is coming for whom, and you suddenly told me you felt much better now. I told you to stay here if you needed to, and I went back to our class."

I looked at her for a moment, "I don't remember you standing next to me . . . Miss Mendez."

"Well . . . I just wanted to make sure you were feeling better, Robert."

I was confused about everything Miss Mendez told me. I do not remember her approaching me inside the restroom or saying anything to her. I could not understand what happened after seeing the little boy outside the window, which seemed so real. Even though I told Miss Mendez I felt better, I really did not feel that much better after leaving her classroom. I could only hope to go through the rest of my day without having to go home early.

The day finally ended as I made my way to the bus to go home. I sat in the far back staring out the window while waiting for everyone to sit down. Unable to forget what happened, I felt relieved to finally start my Christmas vacation but was still feeling confused as I looked out toward the green field. Even though I was leaving behind what I experienced during class, I still had to face what was waiting for me at home as the night started to set in.

Arriving back home, I tried to forget about what happened in school. I knew I could not tell my mother what had happened, knowing how worried she would become. Now I am starting to think about everything I am going through, like the nightmares and the little boy I saw could be made up inside my head. Making me think that something dark has come back to haunt me. At least, that is how I feel, although my family and I went through some strange things two years ago.

To me, nothing was more overwhelming than when my brother was trying to communicate with me after passing away. Somehow, I still felt his presence after moving into this house in the country. Often, I would find myself standing in the middle of the floor surrounded by complete darkness in the far back bedroom. The bedroom would feel so cold and empty, yet I was not alone. Even though I could not see anything, I could hear someone or something moving around on the bed sitting in the corner of the room. After going through this for a while, I started to see a shapeless dark figure moving around in the dark. This experience seemed more like a dream, only catching a glimpse of his image as it disappeared into the darkness while I rubbed my eyes to get a better look. I believed everything that I was facing was a dream of being half-asleep standing in a dark empty bedroom.

Then other things started to happen. I would discover certain items belonging to me were disappearing from the middle bedroom I slept in then suddenly appearing inside the empty back bedroom. Not long after experiencing the images and the misplaced items, I started to hear strange noises in the middle of the night coming from this same bedroom, and I found my things.

One night, upon waking up in the middle of sleepwalking, I found myself standing in the back bedroom looking around in the dark. Already feeling as if someone was here with me, I slowly walked toward the light coming from under the bathroom door. Making my way toward the light, I suddenly hit something with my foot. I noticed my silver Corvette remote-control sitting near the bathroom door. Feeling scared and confused, I quickly went into the bathroom then made my way back to my bed shutting the door behind me. I could not help but wonder why my remote-controlled car was sitting on the floor when I kept it inside my closet up on a shelf.

On other nights, I could barely hear music coming from the clock radio sitting on a small table next to the bed in the back bedroom. Unable to fall back asleep, I would get up from my bed and go turn the clock radio off to keep myself from thinking that someone was there.

One particular night, as I was struggling with the anxiety of going to sleep, I heard the clock radio come on. I got out of my bed and slowly walked into the back bedroom to go turn it off, while looking over at the empty bed. Already having a feeling of someone or something inside this bedroom, I suddenly was staring at my small Bible that I always kept inside the top drawer with my clothes. It was lying on this bed! I grabbed it off the bed and ran back to my room, feeling so terrified.

Night after night, I was experiencing strange things going on late at night inside the empty bedroom; I started to hear noises. I would lie in my bed hearing low creaking sounds, as if someone were walking around inside the back bedroom. Too scared to find out where the noises were coming from, I started to ignore everything around me at night by placing my hands over my ears and covering my head with my blanket.

As time went by, living in this house I still had to face waking up at three in the morning, standing in a dark bedroom feeling air flickering near my ear. As if there were something trying to get my attention. Soon, I started sensing David's presence coming from this bedroom, even though he had never had a chance to move with us after my family and I left the one-bedroom house in town.

It truly seemed as if David had never left us. I felt sad not having a chance to see him again; only noticing the signs of his presence through the strange noises and the things I would find lying around our house. He was still with us during a time when we were adjusting to the loss of moving forward without my brother. I knew we would never see him again, although the memories which remain inside my mind may have caused these vivid images of David to manifest from my dreams into a spirit living in the back bedroom two years ago.

Today, I still feel David here with me, even though his spirit has disappeared. Only the memory remains—watching how happy he looked sitting next to me inside the car when my parents would take us on long trips to the mountains. Now, I can only hope what I am experiencing with the nightmares and the images appearing to me for no reason have nothing to do with David.

Something strange is happening to me. To see an image in the middle of the day as well as not remembering certain things told to me by my teacher. Sleeping in the back bedroom has now forced me to face the same experiences my brother once went through when he was still with us. Now, I must face whatever seems to have returned to possess me through the images and the nightmares like it did with my brother. David became haunted by the images and the nightmares right up to his death, not realizing his experiences may have been warning signs of what was about to happen to him. The dark figure appearing in David's nightmares could have been Uncle Eddie standing over my father, holding a gun to his head leading up to the fatal shooting. The knocking on the wall David heard during the night could have been the same knocking I heard coming from Uncle Eddie. With the gun still in his hand, he paced along the floor while hitting the barrel of the gun against the wall now realizing he had just shot David.

I feel as if this was part of a curse placed upon me and my brother by something so evil, using my Uncle Eddie to take David from us. Now it's coming for me . . . Uncle Eddie's wife, Barbara, had something to do with David's death, knowing her involvement with the practice of Black Magic and hearing the curse placed on us by Uncle Eddie. I seem to think Aunt Barbara wants to finish what my Uncle Eddie started by using her witchcraft to come for me. Not only did Barbara already place a curse on me and my brother, but she also placed a curse on my father, who went over to her house drunk, seeking answers for what Eddie had done.

After my father left her house, he came home feeling sick, thinking it may have been from too many days of drinking. He was unable to eat or drink anything for a while, and we soon found out from Aunt Vera that my father's life was slowly draining from his body by a curse Barbara placed on him when he went over to her house. Little did we know, Barbara also attached an evil entity to follow my father back to our house.

As David's spirit tried to reconnect with its own soul while trapped between an existing and non-existing world, the evil entity tried to take the soul of David while leaving behind his spirit to wander aimlessly forever. Fortunately, Aunt Vera stopped this from happening by using her own White Magic.

I can only hope that I am wrong about facing someone so evil; nevertheless, having my Aunt Vera ready to help us made me feel less afraid of any dark evil energy that wants to take me away from my parents like it did with my brother David.

CHAPTER 4

PASSING

THE FOG COVERS THE WALNUT ORCHARD making it difficult to see our house from the road at night.

Our house sits inside an old walnut orchard that seems to trap all the mysterious dark energy along with an empty, lonely feeling of being the only family living out here in the country, near a paved road torn apart by the tractors used by the local farmers to cultivate their crops. No one seems to drive through the road, which makes me and my mother become overly concerned when a car drives up into our unpaved driveway at night when my father is either asleep or is gone, drinking with his family.

Sometimes, I can hear strange noises coming from outside when I am sitting inside my bedroom late at night trying to avoid looking out my window and staring into the trees, which makes everything around our house look so eerie. Especially in the winter when the night sets in and the fog becomes thick inside the walnut orchard while the huge branches block out the moonlight, trapping all that lurks in the darkness, just waiting for any chance to feed off any fears I may have.

There are moments I sit and think about the people who lived here long ago and wonder what kind of unforeseen tragedy could have led up to this negative feeling inside this house today. Stories told by my family about the house never made living here any easier, knowing what the other people living here before us had experienced; especially now, with what my parents and I went through two years ago. Nevertheless, I must ignore my thoughts about how I feel living here and continue to wait as if I am expecting something bad to happen.

Tonight feels different, even though it is just like any other frigid winter with the fog covering our house and the thoughts of all the mysterious creatures that might be lurking outside hidden behind those trees. My parents are still watching television in the living room while I am inside the back bedroom listening to music from a clock radio that has been sitting inside here before I moved from the middle bedroom. With everything going on with the nightmares and the strange images, I still look around my bedroom expecting any sign of David's presence or something bad returning. Regardless, I had to be ready for about anything. At least, that is what I thought.

The telephone rang and I heard my mother get up to find out who could be calling so late at night. I lowered my music to hear my mother on the phone. Suddenly, I hear her say, "Oh no, this can't be true . . . "

I got up from my bed and walked over to the door leading into the kitchen to listen to what was going on. I could only hear my mother crying as she hung up the telephone. I slowly opened the door, walking through the kitchen into the living room where my parents were sitting. I could see my mother wiping her eyes with the back of her hand and my father sitting in his chair, staring at the television set. Pop turned to look at me with a blank look on his face and I knew something bad had happened. I asked my mom why she was crying. Both my parents stared at me as if they were unsure of what to say. My mother started to sob as she softly said,

"Your Aunt Vera just passed away in the hospital. She got very sick with pneumonia and there was nothing the hospital could do to help her . . . "

The thought of never seeing Aunt Vera again became overwhelming. I felt so much sadness, yet another part of me refused to believe she was *actually* gone. Refusing what I had just heard, I could not believe that Aunt Vera would have suddenly become sick and passed away for no reason. I forced myself to get through the night just to wake up in the morning to cope with the loss of Aunt Vera. Lying in bed and staring at the ceiling with my blanket pulled up over my mouth, my eyes wandered around the room with only the light coming from under the bathroom door. As I started to close my eyes, I could see an image of Aunt Vera standing over me while her mouth moved silently as if she was trying to tell me something. I remembered that same moment when Aunt Vera stood over this same bed two years ago as my parents watched her help David's soul become free from the entity that once tried to drag him into its world. I was not sure if I was having a bad dream as I started to fall asleep, or if she actually appeared before me. I opened my eyes, clearing the image out of my mind as I turned on my side, staring at the clock radio. Still feeling overwhelmed by the loss, I forced myself to sleep without having any more thoughts going through my mind. Feeling exhausted, I started to doze off without having any more vivid images of Aunt Vera as I watched the numbers on the clock radio start to disappear.

Soon after falling into a deep sleep, I woke up to the sound of static coming from the clock radio. Slowly opening my eyes to the complete darkness, I lay on my back feeling disoriented. Unable to see anything, I started to hear the static from the radio go away. I lay in bed feeling strange, as if I had awakened in the middle of a nightmare and not knowing where I was. I closed my eyes, becoming dizzy from this spinning feeling inside my head while I lay in bed. I quickly opened my eyes and noticed this was not a nightmare anymore.

I'm levitating above my bed!

So terrified of what is happening right now!

Frantically looking around with barely any light coming from under the bathroom door, I could see myself lying in bed. The room started to circle in slow motion while my body levitated near the ceiling. Unable to make this disembodied experience go away, everything started to look distorted. The room began to twist and bend as I tried to keep my eyes closed, just waiting for the nightmare to stop. Unfortunately, I could not help myself from opening and closing my eyes as I continued watching the room circle in slow motion. Not having any control of my own body, I could only wait to see what was going to happen next.

Suddenly, these images started to appear, standing against the wall with their blurry disfigured faces making it difficult to see who or what they were. Like shadow figures manifesting from the darkness, only the hellish unclear faces appearing stagnant as they circled right past me unaware of what they wanted. I started to get very cold while having this sinking feeling inside my stomach. I knew at that moment I was falling, but unaware of what was going to happen. Just as I was about to fall back into myself lying on the bed, everything around me started to disappear as the room returned to complete darkness.

Thinking the nightmare was over, I found myself lying on the ground inside the old barn. Feeling unsettled by what had just happened, I could not understand how I ended up there. I got up and slowly walked to the entrance of the barn. Cautiously, I stuck my head out through an opening between the two large wooden doors. Looking around in the dark and feeling scared, I squeezed myself through, quickly running across the dirt driveway into the back porch of our house. I turned the door knob and, surprisingly, the door opened. I quietly walked into my bedroom, shutting the door behind me without making too much noise. Quickly turning on and off the light to change out of my dusty clothes, I noticed my curtain was completely open.

I walked over to my bedroom window to close the curtain and I noticed these small reflections coming from outside the old barn. Hoping not to see anything lurking around in the dark, I continued to stare out my window toward the old barn to see where those reflections were coming from. Suddenly, I saw these large white wings extending out from an opening near the roof of the barn as the moonlight filtered down softly through the broken wood shingles that reflected off the purity of its natural color. In the middle of these large wings were the two small reflections I saw earlier as they positioned themselves on the edge of the large opening overlooking our house. As I began to close my curtain, this mysterious winged creature flew off into the darkness. Having never seen anything like this before, I started to wonder if there was a connection between myself waking up inside the barn and the White Owl I just saw fly into the night.

Nothing made any sense, as everything that I was experiencing seemed to be getting worse with a considerable number of unexpected events starting to show up more, for no reason. Aunt Vera's passing has not made my life any easier with everything I have been going through. However, tonight I experienced so much anxiety along with the fear of not having any control over what is leading me into this dark supernatural world. I can only hope that my Aunt Vera is at peace, watching over us. Just like when she would call us on the telephone to see how we were doing.

Regardless of everything that happened tonight, I need to get to sleep and ignore my own thoughts of trying to make any sense of this. I am hoping that everything I have experienced up to this point is not from something so terrible, just wanting to devour every part of who I am.

CHAPTER 5
THE WOODEN RECORD PLAYER BOX

WAKING UP WHILE SQUINTING and rubbing my face as the sunlight comes through my curtain—a curtain made of an old thin bed sheet covered with water stains from the rain seeping through the opening around the wooden frame—I am exhausted from having little sleep.

I stared at the shadows on the ceiling from the tree branches moving back and forth by the breeze outside my window as the sunlight brightened my bedroom. Thinking about last night, I turned to look at the time on the clock while smelling breakfast prepared by my mother. I got out of bed and went into the kitchen where my mother was sitting down at the table drinking a cup of coffee. She got up to fix me a plate of food while asking if I was doing okay since Aunt Vera's passing. Anticipating that my mother would be concerned about what I experienced last night, I only asked if she knew anything about a white bird flying around our house. My mother squinted while turning her head slightly sideways, displaying a concerned look on her face.

"This white bird . . . did you see it?" she asked.

"Yes . . . looking out from an opening near the roof of the barn last night."

Mom put her head down, looking toward the floor, rubbing her chin, hesitating, unsure of what to say. She lifted her head up and looked right at me, "You must have seen a White Owl . . . my grandfather used to say if a White Owl shows itself during the night over your home, this usually means the owl senses death or a presence of a *lost soul*."

I thought how strange it was to see this White Owl after grieving over the death of Aunt Vera, although I didn't understand how an owl could be something bad when it was just an animal. My mother tried to convince me how serious it was to see a White Owl at night. She saw it as a sign of something bad about to happen to someone living in the home where the owl appears. Regardless of what my mother thought, I only saw a White Owl resting inside the barn.

I finished my breakfast and put my plate in the kitchen sink. I was about to run out the back door when Mom suddenly stopped me. She grabbed my wrist just before walking past her to let me know not to wander off too far. I smiled, letting her know I would be in the backyard. She smiled back, letting go of my wrist as I stood there for a moment before turning around and running out the back door.

Feeling the freezing air hit me as I walked out into the backyard I noticed some fog still lingering around inside the walnut orchard. I walked up to the front of the barn, peering into an opening near the roof where I had seen the White Owl just before it flew off into the dark. As I got closer to the two sliding doors barely hanging off the metal rails, I stood in front of the barn thinking about everything going on living inside our house.

Everything I have experienced so far has become more difficult to understand. Like the images during the day, which appear like day-dreams becoming so real, while the nightmares have opened this door into a dark world allowing all the bad things to pass through at night when I lie down to close my eyes.

I looked back toward our house, feeling confused yet concerned, with everything starting to get worse. I have to wait just to see something terrible appear to me as I become more vulnerable to things that only come out late at night. I can only hope that I am wrong about everything, and not have to face something bad happening to me.

Still standing in front of the large wooden doors, I began to walk along the outside of the barn, making my way into the orchard. I could feel the tiny droplets going into my nose as I breathed in the cold mist from the fog still lingering throughout the trees. So peaceful and quiet, hearing the water drop off the limbs of the old trees around me as I walked farther into the orchard. I started to see something move just ahead of me. Hesitating to go any farther, I waited for a moment to see what could be moving around.

Once again, I began walking through the wet grass while feeling a little uneasy. Suddenly, I caught a glimpse of a shadow-like figure moving from one tree to another. I stopped. Frantically looking to see where the shadow had disappeared, I became too scared to go on. Watching and waiting just to see if it appeared again, I began to notice everything around me becoming quiet. *I don't even hear the water dropping from the tree branches like before*, I thought to myself. The peace I felt earlier walking through the orchard went away, and everything around me started to feel strange. Sensing as if someone or something was watching me, I slowly moved behind a tree, continuing to watch for any movement. I started to notice the dark shadow move out from behind the tree.

OH MY GOD . . . I am looking at the same little boy I saw outside my window when I was sitting in class. The little boy was now standing next to the tree, staring at me. Suddenly bent over, I began vomiting while watching the little boy begin to speak. I fell to my hands and knees, trying to keep myself from completely falling to the ground. I felt my eyes roll back and everything went dark.

Gradually opening my eyes while resting on my back, I could feel the cold ground as I stared up at the tree branches above me. I turned over to push myself up, trying to understand what had just happened. I still felt a little nauseated and scared as I looked around for the little boy. Seeing him again, I was unsure if I was imagining all of this. Especially knowing that I was not the only one who had ever seen him appear in front of me.

Now looking back, Aunt Vera's description of what she saw two years ago inside her motor home when visiting seemed to be what I had now started to see. The same little boy my Aunt Vera believed to be my brother David had returned. Unable to control my emotions, I could not hold back my tears from thinking about David's spirit coming back and suddenly appearing after two years?

Trying to understand what had just happened, I began to walk back to the house while still feeling scared about seeing the image of the little boy. As I walked out of the orchard, I turned around, sensing that someone was following behind me. I kept looking back while quickly making my way to the house. I suddenly stopped at the back door, knocking the dirt off my pants with my hands before going in. I took a deep breath and walked into the house acting as if nothing had ever happened. Rushing right past my mother standing near the kitchen sink, she quickly turned around to ask me where I had been.

"It's after four o'clock and you were gone all day, Robert."

I thought to myself . . . *it was still morning when I saw that little boy by the trees. I can't believe how long I was lying on the ground and still thinking it was morning.*

Not realizing how much time had gone by after passing out, I felt overwhelmed by so much anxiety while holding in the panic coming from my voice. I kept myself from saying anything to my mother about what I experienced back in the orchard. After a moment of trying to figure out what to say, I responded by telling her about how I lost track of time while playing in the orchard. Putting my head down, I was unable to look at her knowing this was not true. My mother looked at me from top to bottom as my father walked into the house from working all day on the ranch. She told me to change my clothes and wash up for dinner.

I slowly began walking to my bedroom trying to forget about everything that had happened, while hoping for these occurrences to stop. I still have to face each night without knowing what is going to happen when I am sound asleep. My life seems to revolve around so many unexplained events. An unsettling fear seems to always stay with me, unaware of what each day has to offer. I cannot seem to close my eyes without something dark taking control of me as it leaves behind the fear and confusion along with a feeling of hopelessness. The same hopeless feeling my brother must have felt when he would see something dark tormenting him up until his sudden death.

Could this be a part of the curse . . . or something supernatural? Unfortunately, I will never understand what has caused this door to open, drawing my existence into a mysterious path as it did with my brother. I can only pray to GOD to give me the strength to face what lies ahead, instead of having to face the fear that once hid inside this house.

Sometimes I want to believe that there could be other reasons behind the images' unexpectedly appearing during the day and at night. Just hoping the images, which seem so real, are coming from memories manifesting into my nightmares; becoming this whole other world made up inside my head.

Still, this does not explain why I cannot remember waking up somewhere else and not knowing how I got there. Even though I try to think my experiences are just inside my head, I have to acknowledge that my vulnerability and anxiety are becoming afflicted by a dark force causing the blackouts that I have been having. I am going through the same experiences my brother once had. Becoming withdrawn from everyone, while having to battle something so dark inside our nightmares. Unlike my brother, I *will* find a way to end this curse that has already inflicted so much pain on my family. I can only hope to stop all this before things start to get worse.

After dinner, my father talked to my mother about going to the fire station in the morning to pick up a Christmas tree. I became excited.

"Can I go with you, Pop?"

He looked at me and smiled, knowing how excited I was. Then getting up from his chair to go into his bedroom, he answered, "Yes, but we will be heading out early."

I could not wait for the morning to arrive, so I decided to turn in early to make sure he did not leave me behind.

I always look forward to every December when our local firefighters go up to the mountains and bring back Christmas trees to sell to the public. Walking around while looking for a tree always reminds me how close we are to Christmas. The food Mom will prepare and the family that stops by to visit during the Christmas holiday always brings happiness into our home, while helping me forget about all the terrible things I must face each day. Nothing brings more joy to our home than placing the lights on the tree and watching all the different colored lights brighten up the room, allowing me to feel happy for the moment.

I suddenly became sad, knowing we no longer would be spending our holidays with David. I walked into my bedroom and sat on my bed, feeling so emotional. I lay down thinking about David and how we used to spend our holidays together. Staring at the ceiling, I began to whisper, "I miss you so much, David . . . I wish you were here with me."

I turned over on my side, looking at the time on the clock, and trying to force myself to go to sleep. I had to get up early enough to go into town with my dad to pick out our Christmas tree. Even though I was excited about tomorrow, I still had this thought in the back of my mind about waking up in the middle of the night just to face another strange occurrence. Sometimes I become frustrated, feeling trapped by the fear of not having control of what is happening to me. Like waking up and finding myself somewhere else other than my bed. Regardless of what might happen tonight, I will have to ignore everything up to this point and try falling asleep.

Just after eight p.m., as I lay in my bed unable to go to sleep, I suddenly started thinking about that White Owl. I got out of bed to look out the window. I could not see too much since the scattered rain started to hit my window. I could smell the damp air coming in through the old frame around the window. I went back to bed, desperately trying to get sleep without thinking about anything. Unfortunately, time kept passing by and I became frustrated. After two hours of moving around under my blanket, I finally fell asleep.

Suddenly, I opened my eyes as if I had just fallen asleep. My stomach was turning as if I needed to vomit. I felt disembodied, staring into the dark, unaware of what I was looking at. My body felt numb, unable to move my arms and legs. I started to feel horrified and panicky at having no control over what was happening to me right at this moment. I could not seem to stop this nightmare. I closed my eyes, trying to ignore what was happening. I felt myself wanting to vomit, while my body started to circle in the darkness. My body was moving in slow motion and the room started to feel shaky and blurry. I suddenly started seeing shadow-like figures all around me. Each pitch-black figure appeared through the darkness as I circled right past them. I started to vomit on myself, ready to pass out while begging for all this to stop.

"Oh God, make this stop, I feel like I'm going to die."

I kept opening and closing my eyes, still seeing each dark figure watching me. The dark figures seemed to be the same one becoming multiple as I circled right past it. I frantically looked away, fearing that this dark shadow wanted to hurt me. I struggled to move my body to end this nightmare. I started to feel a strange coldness come over me while the wet vomit on my chest made me feel even colder. I began to breathe in this cold air as I continued to open and close my eyes, feeling so terrified to be unaware of what was going to happen.

Everything suddenly stopped as I continued to breathe in the cold air. I opened my eyes while lying on my back, staring into the darkness.

I knew from the smell of the dust and the damp cold feeling I was lying on the ground of the old barn. Feeling scared and confused, I sat up, looking toward the moonlight coming in through the opening of a loose board. I got up from the ground while wiping the vomit off the front of my shirt, hoping I would not see that dark figure.

Even though the barn was so dark, I could see something reflecting from where the moonlight was coming in. Feeling a little disoriented, I walked toward it. The reflection seemed so bright from the amount of light shining through, as if something was guiding me, wanting to find it. I still felt scared looking cautiously around in the dark. I stopped to where the reflection was coming from and saw a wooden box sitting on the ground. The reflection was coming off a small metal plate attached to the side of the box. It was difficult to see what the box was with the amount of light coming in, so I had to carry it outside to get a better look. Even considering how dark it was, I needed to see what I was looking at. I picked up the wooden box and walked over to the entrance of the barn. I set it on the ground to see what I could find. I rubbed off the dirt on a small metal plate attached to the side of it. I could see a picture of a dog facing a horn (the RCA Victor Dog). I started to turn the round metal plate on top with my fingers, reminding me of the record player without the horn (Gramophone Record Player) I saw on those old black-and-white movies my father watched on television. The top of this old wooden box seemed to lift. I placed both hands using my fingers to grasp the front just under the round metal plate to lift the top. I noticed a dusty white cloth rolled up inside. I grabbed the cloth and slowly unwrapped it. As I carefully unwrapped the cloth to see what was inside, I felt something small with sharp edges. Unraveling the last wrap of the old dusty rag, I noticed this shiny metal object with two cross arms (The Cross of Caravaca de la Cruz).

I have seen this cross before. My Aunt Vera gave the cross to my brother. David was afraid of the cross and kept it in the top drawer of his dresser in the bedroom. He seemed to fear one just like it, not wanting to upset whatever was haunting him when we lived inside the small one-bedroom house in town.

Suddenly, I heard a noise behind me. Wrapping the cross up with the cloth, I put it quickly inside my front pocket. I closed the box while putting my hand over my nose to keep myself from sneezing. I went back inside and quickly put it back where I found it. Terrified and shivering from the cold air, I could sense something inside the barn with me. I looked around while hearing noises coming from inside the barn. Tapping sounds and creaking noises moving from the walls to the beams above me. I looked up and saw the moonlight barely shining through the opening of the missing wooden shingles. All I could think about was running out of this barn and into my house where I feel much safer.

Feeling confused and scared, my left hand started to lift uncontrollably as if someone was pulling on me. I frantically pulled my hand back and placed it close to my chest. I began to panic, unable to move as something began to touch my left arm. I slowly turned to see what it was.

Oh GOD . . . it was the little boy standing next to me. Horrified, I was unable to run. My legs began to shake, becoming too weak to hold myself up. I suddenly fell to the ground as everything became dark.

Opening my eyes, I can only see the darkness all around me while a chill runs through my body. I lie on my back feeling terrified of what had just happened. I push myself up from the ground, anticipating that the little boy is still here. I look around for the entrance to leave the barn, but I am unable to see through the darkness as I turn in every direction to look for a way out. *"The wooden box . . . the light coming through the loose board. I do not see anything . . . not even the entrance to leave the barn"* Feeling so much anxiety as I desperately look around for a way out through the dark, fear runs through my body as I feel myself wanting to vomit and black out again.

Every time I go through these unsettling experiences, my mind begins to flood with so many unanswered questions, *"What is happening to me? Why am I going through this?"* I have often gone through these experiences without having the understanding or the control of what is happening to me. But I always seem to return from the nightmares and go right back to what I was doing. This time, something was different about all this. This nightmare seemed real, with no way of finding my way back.

Frightened and trapped by the darkness, I needed to look for the entrance. So scared, I couldn't see anything in front of me. I did not see any moonlight coming in to find my way out of this barn. I felt terrified and lost without any way of getting out. I do not know if I am just having a nightmare, or if something has lured me into a mysterious dark place. I am so scared . . . I can hear something moving around me but all I see is darkness. *"Please GOD, help me. Please GOD, I'm so terrified that I don't know what is happening . . . "*

CHAPTER 6
THE DARK PLACE

SLOWLY WALKING and listening for anything wanting to hurt me, I keep looking around hoping to find a way out. Not knowing which way to go keeps me trapped as my eyes try to adjust to this darkness.

An overwhelming fear has come over me, wanting to just give up and accept whatever happens to me. I try to keep myself from becoming more terrified even though the panic has already set in. I cannot seem to catch my breath, *Oh GOD . . .* I feel like I am going to pass out. I close my eyes hoping everything that I am experiencing will stop. Unfortunately, when I open my eyes to see if I am having a nightmare, I find myself still inside this unsettling place. So many emotions going through my mind at this moment that I am unable to suppress this nightmare as I tell myself, *all this can't be real.*

Two small reflections start to appear ahead of me. I feel so scared yet confused about the images appearing inside the darkness only to become abstract to what I believe to be reality. The closer I find myself drawn into this mysterious darkness, the more confused and terrified I become. Unsettling thoughts go through my head while standing here horrified as I try to find my way back. Already terrified, I try to avoid the possibility of something evil waiting and watching just to pull me into its world. I can still feel a cold chill run through my body while my stomach hurts from the anxiety of not knowing what is going to happen next. I keep looking at the two small circular reflections unaware of what they are. I desperately look for any signs of escape. It seems so strange to see the reflections since everything around me is so dark. I have no way of knowing which way to go other than walking toward those reflections.

My ears suddenly become plugged. Only the humming coming from my ears is making everything worse by not being able to hear anything around me. Putting a hand over each ear, I start pushing in and out to get my hearing back. This does not seem to work. I start to panic worse. "What is happening to me . . . ?"

I start to slowly walk around inside the dark holding my head, hoping nothing is going to happen to me. I keep my eyes open even though I cannot see anything in front of me. I begin to feel a sharp pain inside my head as I walk closer toward those two small reflections. I can feel something pulling on my hand again. I could not see anything, but I knew who it was. Suddenly lights appear flickering ahead of me from where the reflections are. With the amount of light just ahead, I can now see where I am going. The pain inside my head has become overwhelming. The thought of running would be impossible since I am walking on a poor-lit path trapped by a wall of darkness without any direction.

Unable to hear anything around me while the pain sustains inside my head, I had to stop from going any farther. I held my head with both hands hoping for all of this to go away. Something suddenly touched the back of my arm. I quickly turned around to find the little boy standing behind me with blood running down the sides of his face. I quickly jumped back screaming but nothing was coming out of my mouth. I bent over, grabbing my knees as I tried to catch my breath from seeing the little boy standing there. I turned to look at him as he pointed in the direction of those same reflections and flickering lights. I noticed the path extending farther into the darkness with every flickering light igniting into an endless world with no end in sight. Still bent over gasping for air, I watched this little boy whom I believed to be David trying to show me something. Having been horrified by what I just saw, I became more overwhelmed by so much sadness of having to remember the night when I last saw him. As he stood before me with blood coming down his face, I became reminded of the night I stood at the foot of his bed, watching our mother hold onto him while his blood ran down her nightgown—the bullet discharge from Uncle Eddie's gun.

I finally stood straight up looking to where he was pointing, trying to keep myself from remembering any more things about the tragic night of David's death. But those memories seemed to come back again by seeing him here with me.

I'm *remembering* . . . suddenly awakened by a loud noise, I heard voices inside the bedroom. I heard my father talking to someone standing over him. It was very dark in the bedroom that David and I shared with our parents when we lived inside the one-bedroom house in town. I was so frightened trying to listen to what was going on. I could hear the whispering coming from my father and this dark figure standing over him. I looked over at my brother and saw this shadow-like figure above David as he stared toward the ceiling. This shadow-like figure looked like the one David would draw on a piece of paper when he became withdrawn and distant from me and our parents. The shadow-like figure hovered above David having full control of him. I turned back to look at my father with this dark figure standing over him, suddenly hearing a voice say, *"I curse one of your kids to die in seven years."*

I heard Pop say, "Eddie, put your gun down and go home . . . you're drunk."

This dark figure, whom I found out later to be Uncle Eddie, held a gun to my father's head. Uncle Eddie's voice had become louder and a struggle started between them. My mother, who was lying next to my father, yelled and told them to stop. I became frightened looking over to where David was. My brother was whispering as he stared at the ceiling while this dark shadow-like figure stood over him. David then turned to look at me, and I could not forget how his eyes looked when he stared right at me. His eyes were completely black and sunken in, as if something evil were draining the life out of him. Simultaneously, I heard a gunshot and saw Mom run over to David. I got out of my bed and stood at the foot of David's bed, watching my mother scream in horror as my brother lay lifeless in her arms. David's . . . eyes were still open looking at me.

Something strange had happened to David before his tragic death. I saw something with him that night, but I was unsure what I was looking at. Something dark had attached itself to David and started to change him before his death. Something evil sent Uncle Eddie over to our house to take David away from us. Something sinister was controlling Uncle Eddie by using him to help drag my brother into its dark world. I seem to think that the curse my Uncle Eddie placed on this family is still haunting us. Looking back to the night of the incident standing at the foot of David's bed, I do remember noticing a dark, shadow-like figure ascending as David lay lifeless in our mother's arms. So much was going on that night all around me that whatever it was I saw over David must have left after it got what it wanted; what it came for.

Why would I forget about seeing the dark shadow figure over David until now? This disturbing image of my brother standing before me at this moment must be a sign. I looked behind me and his image was gone. I called out his name, "David . . . David, where are you?" He was nowhere to be seen.

Once again, I began walking toward the flickering lights near the two reflections. Looking around very carefully, I could see the circular reflections become larger as I got closer. This place felt cold and dreary. I could smell a terrible stench coming from the air, making it difficult for me to breathe in. The stench of rotted mold was starting to leave a strange, bitter taste in my mouth. I found it difficult to keep my mouth closed from uncontrollably shaking from the cold air and fear running through my body. I continued to get closer to the lights as I felt myself pulling away from my own world into a place that seemed more terrifying than my nightmares. A place filled with unforeseen entities which manifest into dark images. A path filled with nothing but darkness devouring the lost souls of those who become lost in an empty, dreadful world. The same path, trapping the most vulnerable like myself by driving away the spirit from our own existence as it pushes us farther away from the only world we have ever known into infinite darkness.

Something evil has dragged me here, watching and waiting while I wander aimlessly farther—and deeper—into their clutches. There must be a reason for me waking up and finding myself inside this place. Was deception by something evil used to drag me down this dark path? If I was not inside the old barn anymore, *where am I?* And *why am I here?*

I am unable to see anything on either side of me, only the dim light flickering ahead. The reflections are coming from the middle of the path surrounded by flickering lights sitting along the ground on each side creating this poorly lit pathway into the darkness. As I get closer, I begin walking between these glass candles with biblical pictures on each one. The same glass candles my mother collects and uses for the nights when the power goes out during a bad storm.

Slowly approaching those reflections, I begin to see a large white creature on the ground of the pathway with its eyes glaring at me. This creature looks like the White Owl that stood outside our house watching from an opening near the roof of the old barn, except now *much* larger. I got scared of getting any closer while remembering seeing the White Owl from before.

I would look out my bedroom window and see a White Owl watching our house from the old barn. I never gave any thought to why I would see the "White Owl," which is what I now call it, with its glaring eyes facing the direction of our house. The only other person aware of the White Owl was my Aunt Vera, when she and Uncle Joe came by to visit. That night, they had their motor home parked in the backyard. Aunt Vera woke up in the middle of the night and saw a small shadow-like figure standing in the middle of the hallway of the motor home. After asking what the spirit wanted, Aunt Vera watched it disappear. When she got up to walk out of her motor home into our house, she saw a large, white-winged creature fly over her as it disappeared into the night.

Aunt Vera sensed that there was a connection between David's spirit and the white-winged creature. She walked quietly into the house and saw my mother going back into her bedroom. Aunt Vera called her over to the kitchen to tell her what she saw. Aunt Vera also mentioned seeing something white fly over her as she walked out of her motor home. She believed it to be a White Owl connected to David. Aunt Vera also believed the White Owl had sensed a lost soul coming from this house. She needed to help put David's spirit to rest. His spirit had attached itself to me and my family after the tragic night of his death. David's spirit followed us from the one-bedroom house in town to the ranch.

Aunt Vera knew she needed to help my family. Unfortunately, other strange things happened that night. Something dark and evil had rendered its curse on my family and tried to take David's spirit along with his soul. The practices of Aunt Vera's White Magic allowed my brother to be set free from the darkness that attached itself to my family. It was not until I started to go through the same strange experiences with the nightmares as my brother had, that I started to see the White Owl outside our house. Something has led me here facing the White Owl that once sensed the lost soul of my brother. Did my brother experience what I am going through now? Two worlds crossing with no boundaries between reality and the supernatural? I feel lost walking through this empty dark place, no way of finding my way back. With the darkness all around me, I fear that the White Owl is not the only thing here with me.

Suddenly, I saw these large white wings spread open like an angel coming down from the heavens to save me. I continued to stare at this beautiful creature, but something strange was starting to happen. Everything around me began to look distorted, causing me to panic. I started to become dizzy as I watched the wings of this White Owl move in a slow, wavy motion. Just like a nightmare, my body felt weightless as I started to drift off, watching these large wings move up and down. As if I am leading one nightmare into another. I cannot stop what is happening, overcome by a feeling of numbness throughout my body. I can barely see the White Owl as its wings move slowly up and down. My eyes roll back as I watch everything around me become pitch-black.

CHAPTER 7
REMEMBERED THOUGHTS

STARING INTO THE DARK as I lay in bed, the rain was coming down, hitting the bedroom window of our small one-bedroom house in town. My parents sleep on the other side of the bedroom from me and David. I whispered, "David, David, David . . . are you asleep?"

"No . . . I can't sleep," he answered.

David suddenly turns over to look at me, "Listen Robert . . . if I tell you something, don't tell Mom or Pop."

"Okay . . . I won't say nothing."

David hesitates for a moment to tell me. I became impatient as my whispers grew louder, wanting to know what my brother was going to tell me. "Okay . . . okay, be quiet, Robert. Well . . . I have woken up at night seeing things and it really scares me."

"What do you see?" I asked.

"Well . . . I see dark figures watching me. I wake up in the middle of the night and see them standing over me. I can't see their faces. I get so scared that I can't move. I start to scream but nothing seems to come out of my mouth. I'm so scared, Robert."

"David . . . Don't be scared. I will always protect you."

David pulled his blanket over his head and told me goodnight. I knew something was wrong with David. Later, he would become withdrawn, never leaving his bedroom. Sometimes I would go into our bedroom just to see what he was doing. He would be mumbling to himself while drawing these pictures. I would ask him what he was doing and he would not say anything. I could see David drawing these dark figures that seemed very scary. The same dark figures that would appear to him at night. David would ignore me and continue what he was doing when I asked him if that was what he saw at night. I would walk out of the bedroom, having no idea what was happening to him. Even though David continued to become distant from us, I knew I still had my brother.

Days went by and he continued to have this faraway look in his eyes. I would look at him and see someone else; he was not David anymore. Something had taken him from us. Something he saw each night standing over him, the shadow-like figures he often spoke about and feared so much. I started to feel sad thinking about how we used to do things together as David continued to keep himself away from everyone. All I could think about was having my brother back, but that is when the unthinkable happened. I felt responsible for not protecting my brother as I watched him being taken away in an ambulance, never returning to us again.

I cried and cried for my brother as I felt this sinking feeling, along with an overwhelming pain in my stomach. I cannot forget how he looked at me with the fear still on his face while he was being carried away in the ambulance. It was as if he died with the same look I saw as I was watching him draw those dark figures. The fear I saw seemed to slowly devour every part of who he was. Trapped by the shadow-like figures circling him like a carousel in the night, only to devise its evil intent to tear this family apart. I would never have imagined my brother leaving us forever, but something had taken him that night. I believed something dark had placed a curse using Uncle Eddie to complete its insufferable purpose.

The pain of losing my brother as I lie in bed each night continues to haunt me. Saddened by so many thoughts of what he must have gone through during those last hours of his life, and not knowing he would be leaving us forever. I never knew what he was *actually* experiencing the last moment before leaving this world. I am only left with the same unanswered questions: Was David still my brother when I last saw him? Or did something from his nightmare already take him from us?

The night of the tragedy, before going to sleep, he sat on his bed staring at a piece of paper. His spirit was already becoming weak, overtaken by fear. I knew from looking at him he saw something that made him terrified. I could not see what he saw, only the fear coming from someone who was staring into the face of something very disturbing. I can still see David's eyes from that moment when he looked up at me for the last time and I felt the fear coming from his eyes.

After David's death, we moved from our one-bedroom house in town into a house in the country to be closer to our father's new job. Unfortunately, moving out to the country where Pop began his job of taking care of a local farm just outside Hanford, California, turned out to be the beginning of an unsettling time of my childhood. Most nights I would find myself waking up, standing alone in the dark, swearing I could sense David here with me. It is like David had never left us, yet I felt a strange coldness lingering all around me. A coldness coming from something else inside this house with me, something other than my brother's presence.

I could not understand what was happening to me. I would often sleepwalk repeatedly each night, always finding myself inside this back bedroom. There would be nights that my mother could hear me walking around the house or find me standing in the dark inside the kitchen near the back bedroom. My parents often spoke about my sleepwalking but never pursued taking me to receive any help. The school sent me home with letters indicating the problems I had keeping up with the other kids. Of course, my parents felt I would be okay without seeing a doctor.

One afternoon, a gentleman called to our house to set up an appointment to have my parents take me to his office to see him. My parents were upset. They knew they had no choice but to do what my school advised them to do. At that point, I knew I could not tell him anything, fearing he would take me away from my parents and put me away in a hospital or something. I knew I had to keep quiet and try to get through this. I was so scared and thought about what I was going to tell this strange man when the time came to see him.

A week later, it was near the end of my class and I was ready to go home. It was close to three o'clock and I started to gather my stuff. Suddenly, our principal, Mr. Davis, walked into the classroom to tell me to stay after school. He told me he had informed my parents about an appointment made by the school's therapist located inside this building. I thought this was strange because my parents were supposed to take me to an office instead of Mr. Davis taking me. Once I gathered my stuff, he asked me to follow him down the hallway of the school. I never felt so scared, which made the trip much longer as I tried to keep myself calm from being nervous. I finally approached the office with the principal and this tall man stood up from behind his desk.

"Hello, I'm Dr. Edwind Scott . . . I'm so glad to meet you, Robert."

"Hello . . . " I said quietly, staring at Dr. Scott.

As Mr. Davis was leaving, he said, "Let me know when you are all done, and I will come back to take Robert home."

Dr. Scott waved to Mr. Davis while looking at me with his large eyeglasses, asking me to sit down. Dr. Scott then sat in his chair pulling himself close to his desk. He started tapping on his desk with his fingers while staring at me as if he were waiting for me to say something. After he paused for a moment, he said, "Well . . . your teacher said you're having some trouble in class, is that true, Robert?"

"A little . . . but I can do better," I said.

Then Dr. Scott said, "I spoke to your mother on the phone, and she tells me about your sleepwalking at night."

I just stared at Dr. Scott, unable to respond to what he said by putting my head down. I felt like I was going to be in trouble if I told him anything about my brother or waking up standing in the middle of the back bedroom in the middle of the night. I felt as if he would have my parents send me away.

Dr. Scott said, "You can tell me anything, Robert. Everything we talk about will be between you and me, I promise. You know, I used to sleepwalk when I was a young boy and find myself standing near the kitchen window looking out into our backyard in the middle of the night. I would see things at night that I could not see during the daytime. I was so scared, but I did not tell anyone what I saw. You see, Robert . . . this little boy would appear to me at night standing outside in the backyard. I would become so frightened and run back into my bedroom. This went on for a while until one night I woke up standing near the kitchen window facing toward the backyard, and I did not see him in the backyard like I normally did. I turned away from the window to go back into my bedroom and the same little boy was standing right next to me. I was so terrified to see him pointing out toward the window. I ran as fast as I could to my room and jumped under my blanket, shaking from being so scared.

"The next morning, I took my mother's garden trowel, which looks like this small hand-held shovel, to dig holes around the backyard. Still thinking about what I saw last night, I continued digging around looking for worms. While sitting on the grass, I noticed something shining inside the soil. I cleared the dirt around it while trying to see what I found. As I cleared the dirt, I finally pulled this metal object from the dirt, which was a necklace with a small locket, rusted from being inside the dirt for so long. I ran to the faucet by our house and washed the dirt off to get a better look. I looked at this locket as I turned it over to see if I could open it up to look inside. As I opened the locket, I saw a picture of this little boy. Suddenly, I dropped it on the ground, so I quickly looked down to pick it up and it was gone. I was so confused because I never found the necklace, as if it just disappeared.

"As time went by, news broke out in our small town about an old police case about a mother and her son found murdered in their backyard. The police, who had been investigating this terrible crime for a while, found the father responsible for killing his wife and son. You are probably wondering why I am telling you about this story of a father who did this to his family. Well . . . that same family lived in the very same home that my parents bought years later where I experienced those scary things. I knew the little boy I saw in the backyard was the same boy who died years ago. The locket I dropped was the same locket his mother wore when the newspaper showed a picture of her and her son when they arrested the father later.

"What I realized later was that the little boy was trying to tell me something. I became terrified when I woke up in the middle of sleepwalking and found myself staring out the window looking at a little boy in the backyard. I never thought that this little boy who was standing in the backyard was trying to tell me anything. Everything that I experienced was meant for a reason, just like finding that necklace. I never knew why that man hurt his family. I just know certain things happen to us for a reason. We become this connection to things that you and I can only see, and sometimes this can be scary.

"Remember, Robert, I am always here to help you. We are alike . . . and I know what you are going through. I must let you know, Robert, (pointing at my chest) never hold stuff in too long because you will eventually surround yourself with really bad things that will keep you from being happy. You must never hold anything inside like I did. You need to tell someone.

"Remember . . . Robert . . . Robert . . . *look* at me, I can help you get through any nightmares that you may have."

I lifted my head and asked Dr. Scott, "What . . . whatever happened to the little boy you saw in the backyard?"

Dr. Scott replied, "Well . . . after the necklace mysteriously disappeared, I never saw the little boy again. The necklace was not meant for me to hold onto. Only a 'sign' that the mother and her son were okay. Remember, Robert . . . holding on to things inside could also affect you, like your sleepwalking or having nightmares. Robert . . . I know you had a brother who went through the same things, but you might be emulating what you saw when your brother was still with you and your family. You could be making yourself think that there are things at night bothering you and you do not realize it. This could force you to believe you are going through the same things that you saw your brother go through. Now, if the tragedy of losing your brother is not causing your nightmares and sleepwalking, we are dealing with something much more. Please, Robert, come to my office anytime if you need anything."

I looked at Dr. Scott and thought about what he said. I was still unsure about telling him what was happening to me, so I continued to stay quiet. He already knew about what I was going through. Just as I was going to ask Dr. Scott about the man with the little girl and boy in the picture hanging on the wall behind him, Dr. Scott picked up the phone and called Mr. Davis to come to his office to take me home.

Dr. Scott looked at me again and said, "Remember, Robert, there could be a reason for what you are going through. You could be a connection to something out there using you, like the little boy who used me. One more thing . . . I am sure I will see you again."

Mr. Davis opened the door and I followed him to his car. I sat in the front seat staring out the window, thinking about what Dr. Scott said. I became more confused about what was happening to me after listening to the doctor. I just could not tell him anything, even though he went through the same things when he was young. I thought about my nightmares, how I would levitate above my bed and see these dark figures circling me. How could I be a connection to something so terrifying and unsettling when I only become overwhelmed with fear and anxiety?

If what I am experiencing is just from the pain of losing my brother, why does this nightmare seem so real? If my experiences end up not being the cause of everything that I have gone through, what does Dr. Scott mean when he said I would be facing something much more?

I continued staring out the window with this faraway look, watching the trees go by. I looked at the kids running around in their front yards as we drove by. I could see how happy they looked, chasing each other around their yard. I can only imagine how happy they must be. Laughing and running around with their hands raised high toward the sky as rain started to fall and their parents yelled from the front porch for them to come inside.

The rain started to hit the window as the rivulets of water blurred my vision, keeping me from seeing anything else while looking out. Watching the rain hit the window seems to make everything difficult to see, like the thoughts that go through my head, which have become unclear as I look out into the world that I must live in. Like the rain, everything so far is unclear, becoming just a blur.

CHAPTER 8
THE MESSAGE

I OPEN MY EYES waking up from what seemed to be a dream, only to find myself lying on my back looking up into the darkness without a clue of what just happened.

Exhausted from the fear and anxiety that I have already faced. I have walked this dark, endless path for a while only watching a White Owl become motionless like a dream as I continue to go through this nightmare. I have become angry, wanting to know what has brought me here to suffer in such a dark and lonely place. I have yet to understand what my purpose in life is, since my life has just begun. Everything up to this point has been just unwanted visions connected to my memories and nightmares.

I cannot seem to stop what is happening, but I need to find a way to escape from this nightmare. This dreadful path has already started to consume me by keeping me from finding my way back to my family. My stomach hurts so bad from my body shaking, I do not know if I am terrified or freezing from the cold. I feel as if I am lying on top of something instead of finding myself lying on the ground like the first time waking up inside the barn. I move my hands around underneath me to feel what I am lying on top of, while looking around in the dark for any signs of the White Owl before passing out. I rub my eyes focusing on where I am.

Suddenly, I remember seeing and talking to Dr. Scott when I am out lying on the ground. I started to panic. Where was I? I cannot see or hear anything. *Did I die . . . ?* I sat up looking around to run away but I could not see where I was going. Realizing I could not find my way out, I listened for any noises that could help me find my way around. I started to smell lavender, like the flowers my mother takes to my brother's grave. "Could I be closer to getting out of here?"

Although, something about all this seems strange. Thinking that my mother could be near, I started to yell to get her attention. Nothing . . . I do not hear any response. I quit calling my mother's name fearing that something else could be lurking around inside this dark place. I started to see a dim light appear from where I was sitting. From where the light appeared, I started to see an empty room with barely any light. I saw a man who looks like Dr. Scott appear, sitting in the corner of the room on a chair with a little boy standing next to him, and the little boy is pointing. I looked behind me in the direction of where he was pointing, and I began to feel a chill go through my body. I slowly got up from where I was sitting to go toward the light.

Suddenly, a wind blew right past me. I stopped, and a dark shadow quickly followed behind, going right past me into the darkness on the other side of the room from where Dr. Scott is sitting. Suddenly, from out of the darkness, the large White Owl moved into the dim light. The White Owl walked across the room going right past Dr. Scott and the little boy. Their faces looked empty and soulless without any expression as their heads followed the White Owl going past them to where I was. I knew this was the same owl I saw before passing out. As the White Owl started to come closer to me with its wings still extended, I kept my distance. As I watched in a daze while feeling nervous, the White Owl began to fold its wings back, finally stopping in front of me. We stood staring at each other for a moment, and I felt a sense of comfort coming from this creature. The owl looked directly at me while moving its head from side to side, as if it was trying to understand who I am. I was so scared, yet I knew the White Owl was not here to hurt me.

I asked, "Are you are here to help me find my way back home?"

The White Owl continued to look at me as if I were talking to myself. I put my head down, my voice beginning to sound shaky from the fear and frustration of not getting a response. I started to yell at the White Owl, wanting to know what it wanted, if it were not here to help. My frustration soon turned into sadness, causing me to start crying. The sadness I felt inside from having been through so much in the past seems to return when something bad happens to me. My pain becomes stronger than the fear that follows me inside this nightmare.

Dr. Scott is right. *I'm just making myself believe I'm going through the same things David once went through when he was alive. Everything is happening because I miss my brother, and nothing will ever be the same again.*

Wiping my eyes with the back of my hands, I pulled my shirt up to my face to clean my nose from sniffling and crying. Yet, the owl did not move, its eyes continuing to follow me as I turned to pace back and forth, feeling so frightened and frustrated while talking under my breath, "Why are you here . . . ? What do you want . . . ?"

The White Owl suddenly extended its large wings and took flight into the darkness. I looked at the owl disappear, feeling confused as to why it continues to follow me. I soon forgot what its purpose was while being more concerned about wanting to get out of here. I looked toward Dr. Scott and the little boy to see if they were still inside a room that seemed to appear out of nowhere. I only noticed the dim light opening the path into an empty darkness. Once again, I found myself being led by a bunch of glass candles that seemed to disappear into another place without any sense of hope. I began to follow the flickering lights unaware of where I was going.

Walking along a dim path while carefully looking around, I listened for any noises coming from the pitch-black walls surrounding me. Sensing I was not alone, I kept thinking about the White Owl and what its purpose was.

The White Owl was truly real as I stood directly in front of it. I sensed a strange connection between us as I became emotional while overwhelmed by its presence. As I stared at the White Owl, I tried to catch my breath as the air became thin. I suddenly cried as the pain I felt seemed to leave from inside my stomach. My tears would not stop from the sadness I had carried with me.

The White Owl had given me something I was missing, a sense of peace I felt when David was alive. Strange as everything seemed, all my fears were gone at that moment. I suddenly thought about the scent of lavender I smelled earlier. It seemed to dissipate when the White Owl disappeared, leaving behind the smell of old dust. I wondered if everything I experienced with my emotions, the lavender scent and the images of Dr. Scott and the little boy were all signs given to me by David. Or . . . just random visions made up of memories.

I still felt as if I was inside the "Old Barn" with its dust lingering in the air. Yet, lost within its walls, this dark world had opened a path to the surreal images and unsolicited memories I have only seen in my nightmares. This path has led me into this dark endless realm as it draws me further and further away from my world. Everything about this place is so terrifying. I continue to follow the dim light which shines throughout this dark path. Walking aimlessly, I stared at each glass candle placed along the ground. Each glass candle perfectly placed with a different biblical figure on each one, just like the same candles my mother would light up with a match when our house lights go off during a winter's storm. Someone must have placed those glass candles to purposely mimic my life, forcing me to face this nightmare which seems to revolve around my own existence. Becoming lost . . . like a soul stuck in the afterlife, apart from not being dead. So why am I here . . . ?

Watching out for anything unexpectedly appearing, like the White Owl that follows me. I have heard stories about the White Owl from my parents. Stories told about a White Owl who turns into a witch that wonders throughout the night watching those who are close to death or drawn in by the unrest soul lost between two worlds. Could this be true? My Aunt Vera did see the White Owl fly over her that night right after an apparition appeared inside her motor home. Now, a White Owl stays near the top of an opening of the old barn watching our house at night and then disappears into the night. Again, I am not dead, nor an unrest soul stuck between my world and "some other" dark world. I do not see any reason I would become haunted by all this happening to me. I am very much alive while looking at my breath exhale out of my mouth as I try to find my way out of this horrifying place I have somehow fallen into.

Passing each lit glass candle, I started to hear strange noises all around me. The sound of people whispering from all directions. I could barely hear what was said. Wait . . . I heard something, something coming from the darkness just ahead of me. Whipping sounds getting closer. Suddenly a strong wind blew right past me, and I saw the White Owl land in front of me again. This time it had something in its mouth and laid it on the ground.

With its wings still extended, it flew off into the darkness. I slowly walked over to see what was placed on the ground. A paper folded into a small square. I slowly opened the paper to see what it was. *OMG* . . . shaken by what I was looking at, I stared into the darkness where the owl disappeared, trying to figure out why it left this here. I could not believe what I was holding in my hand, the only thing that

I last saw when my brother was alive. Why . . . why am I holding a drawing of his . . . ?

I remembered watching David draw these pictures of dark shadow-like figures that would appear to him at night. I stood by his side watching as he sat on his bed shut out from everything and everyone around him. Nevertheless, I still felt confused about the drawing placed on the ground and what it meant. I put my head down and thought about what my reason for being here was, to become lost like my brother forever. From what I saw that night, fear had taken over my brother. Seems as if his life was stolen by the dark figures on this paper, which manifested into this form of dark energy through the nightmares devouring all of what was left of him. Without reason, this evil would have no sympathy, emotions, or sorrow for causing my brother's death. Intentionally trying to take over such a vulnerable soul, while callously leaving behind the memories which still linger inside my head. Only forcing upon a sadness that turns into an empty hole in my stomach.

Fear always seems to take over any emotions during a time when I want to give up, but the strength that was placed upon me was given by those who are close. If there is a reason for what I am going through, then show what is in front of me. Present yourself. Stop leaving signs that have led me far from my family into a world watched over by an owl that has not done anything to help me find my way home. *GOD* . . . please help me, please . . .

My body has become numb from this travesty of hope which spares no victims as I stand vulnerable to all that lurks around me. The darkness hides all that waits while I move aimlessly to nowhere; however, the light is the only thing that I can follow in any hope of finding a way out of this place. Turning to the right and then to the left, I could not decide which way to start walking in a place hidden with no direction and poorly lit candles.

I started to fold the drawing and put it in my front pocket with the cross I found earlier inside the wooden box. Not thinking about what all this meant, I began walking on a path drifting into endless darkness. Forced to stay within the boundaries of its imaginary walls. This nightmare seems to keep me moving further into an unsuspecting dreadful place. I can only wonder what hides inside along these dark walls as I unexpectedly wait for something bad to happen. Like a nightmare . . . a nightmare that does not seem to go away.

Is this what my brother David went through when he was alive . . . or when he died becoming a lost soul stuck between both worlds? Is this what he experienced when he was a lifeless soul, wondering, without any meaning or reason for his own existence?

I will never allow myself the chance to find out. I already feel the fear, anxiety, and frustration that make me sick to my stomach.

Fear . . . I feel nothing worse than being denied the waking up from a terrifying nightmare that continues to keep me trapped within this place. Anxiety . . . forced to face this nightmare without any cause or warning by something bad that has led me here. Frustration . . . unable to control what is happening to me, hindering me from living a life free from the "Evil" that forced its way into my world.

So many thoughts repeatedly going through my mind. I try to keep my eyes looking forward, avoiding everything around me. A cold breeze passes right by me; my body starts to shake uncontrollably. I cross my arms and hunch over to keep myself warm. I slowly come to a stop as my eyes shift from one side to the other. I look around, turning in every direction, desperately hoping the White Owl has come back.

The air has changed, colder than before. The lights along the path begin to flicker more than usual, and an awful stench fills the air. I turn my head sideways facing down to the ground, holding my nose. Watching my breath each time I exhale, I try to keep myself from breathing in the unpleasant smell lingering in the air. Something strange is happening . . . *leave me alone! I want all this to stop . . . leave me alone!* I put my head down simultaneously whispering to myself, "I just want to go home." Yet, my attention draws to the smell that reeks of mold and garbage from the trash. Something does not feel right. Whatever went right past me earlier could be anything other than the White Owl. Something feels different. Frustrated yet scared, all I can do is just wait and think about all the unsettling thoughts going through my mind. The possibility that something horrifying can appear at any moment. How much do I have to endure before anything starts to make sense? I find this difficult, having to go on living this nightmare that does not seem to end.

Suddenly remembering the nights staring out my bedroom window, just before going to bed, I looked up into the sky peering at all the lights as far as I could see. Becoming an endless illusion of all the stars reflecting erratically among each other as if they were connected somehow. A never-ending speckle of lights disappearing into the darkness. Every boundless light that seems to fade into this other dark world, opening a mysterious pathway into the unknown.

I have been led into this darkness to fade away like the stars. Unable to see beyond this path. Only the fear and sadness of being alone remains. Yet . . . driven by hope, I continue to find my way home through an endless illusion of flickering lights somehow connecting me to the other things along this path. Unfortunately, fear overruns my thoughts with all the terrifying things that may be hiding within the dark walls surrounding me. Just like the night sky, every boundless flickering light fades into this other dark world. Opening a mysterious pathway into the unknown I now must face.

The only difference between me and the stars: my connection may be with dark figures David drew on a piece of paper. Unlike the stars, which support each other to form a peaceful world within the darkness.

CHAPTER 9
DARK FIGURE

SHIVERING FROM THE COLD, I looked around, frightened by the images that appeared like flashes that pop up from the corner of my eyes.

Delusional from fear, I grabbed the cloth from inside my front pocket to clear my eyes to focus on what was around me. Suddenly panicking, I forgot about the cross wrapped up inside the cloth. I rubbed the cloth with my fingers, hoping I did not drop the cross on the ground. Nothing . . . *I lost the cross*. I bent down on the ground to find it. I started to smell the scent of lavender in the air while moving my fingers throughout the dirt to see if I could find it.

Desperately searching for the cross, a tennis shoe appeared next to my hands. I quickly fell back, sitting on the ground looking up at this little boy wearing corduroy pants and a sweater. My eyes opened wide from the image of this little boy looking directly at me as I stood there horrified. This little boy, whom I recognize to be my brother David, is pointing off into the distance. I slowly got up from the ground to see what he was pointing at. Appearing just ahead of me, I saw a shadow-like figure partially showing itself from within the wall of darkness. I became terrified, watching this dark figure from a distance unaware of what it wants. Suddenly, the little boy bent down and pointed toward the ground. I could see something shining from where he was pointing. The little boy stood up and backed away. I slowly went over to where he was, while looking toward the dark figure still watching from a distance. I fell to the ground on my knees and saw the cross sitting there. Grabbing it with my fingers, I carefully wiped the dust off to wrap it back up inside the cloth. I stuffed the cloth firmly inside my front pocket, making sure I would not lose it again. While the scent of lavender began to go away, I looked around, now not seeing the spirit of my brother anywhere. I was relieved to have found the cross, especially knowing what it meant to me.

This similar cross was given to him for his own protection by my Aunt Vera. Somehow, she knew all the bad energy coming from inside the darkness was waiting and watching as he slept. My Aunt Vera placed the cross in his hand when she stopped by to visit. However, David refused to keep the cross, unaware of the nightmares he was experiencing would soon manifest, overtaking his thoughts and emotions. He was unaware of the fear that would eventually become unbearable, keeping him from living a happy, normal childhood. David was unable to understand what was happening. The signs were unseen by those around him. Overwhelmed by so much fear, frustration, and anxiety, he fell into this world that was not easy to cope with. Something wanted to keep him unprotected, something that would not allow him to hold onto the cross to keep the fear away. Something was provoked by a symbol of peace and salvation given to him by the only person who saw what others could not see. The dark figures placed so much fear inside David, who saw the cross as something bad. He believed that something that was supposed to be a symbol of protection actually provoked all the evil things daunting him late at night.

Ironic as this may seem, I feel safe holding onto the cross, especially knowing my brother's spirit came back to help me find it. This cross must have meant something as he knelt on the ground to show me. I was frightened until l saw his eyes. His eyes gleamed as he smiled, letting me know everything was okay. He smiled like the day I saw him stare out of the car window when my parents took us on a trip to the mountains.

I saw how happy he looked that day. He pointed and smiled as we drove through the mountains, passing every huge tree becoming smaller as we looked farther into the distance. I saw him laughing as he tried to look through the openings between the trees blocking the river along the road. He moved his head side to side as Pop slowly turned with every curve, driving upward into the mountains.

One time when Pop stopped to let us out of the car to look around, David called out to me as he ran toward the trees. He waved his hands for me to follow behind him. I yelled, "Wait for me!" I watched his face light up. I somehow knew he had found his peace.

Just like the way he looked at me pointing toward the missing cross, smiling as his face started to glow. Soon, I felt myself breathing heavily as my tears started to fall down my face. I cannot help but always feel the pain of losing my brother. I will never see his smile again, only the memories of all the times we spent together.

Suddenly, I find myself standing here inside this stupid place, once again facing the same memories that seem to never go away. But, there must be a connection between the cross and the spirit of my brother. I honestly believe the cross inside my pocket belongs to him. That is why he wanted me to find it.

Wiping the tears with the back of my hands, I start to become impatient just waiting for something to happen. A ratchet smell starts to linger, causing me to believe that something dreadful is about to happen. The air has become oddly cold. A light mist is starting to hover right over me as it moves through this poorly lit pathway. I can see the mist coming from where the dark figure is still watching me as it leans out from the darkness. Frightened of what waits ahead, I find myself unable to move from the fear that has completely taken over. A chill starts to run through my body. I start to shake uncontrollably as I watch this horrific image moving into the light. The dark shadow-like figure is now standing with its upper body bent, surrounded by the mist that circles slowly behind it, like two rings rotating in different directions. The dark image moves in a slow, back-and-forth, twisting motion. I watch this pitch-dark figure created from a dark world, expelling these thin translucent waves of black smoke from its black translucent gown as it hovers close to the ground. Long black strands of hair are waving into the air, floating straight up above its shoulders.

Horrified by this faceless Dark Entity, I turn away to begin running as fast as I can. Suddenly, the candles that had kept this pathway lit start to flicker behind me. I panic but my legs become numb as I try to run away.

"OH MY GOD!" Please help me . . . I do not want to see it. I am so scared . . . Everything seems to have gotten worse inside this nightmare. I just want to go home and sleep in my own bed. I look back and the dark figure starts to move toward me. Terrified, I continue desperately to try to get away, and a strong draft suddenly hits my back. So scared, I start to pray that the Entity is not behind me. I look over my shoulder and see the White Owl landing just behind me. The White Owl's wings fold back. The Entity, which had manifested from deep inside the pathway, suddenly stops. The Dark Entity hovers in place as it watches me from a distance. I stop to catch my breath, suddenly remembering where I saw that Dark Entity before. I stuck my hand inside my front pocket to look at the drawing that was placed in front of me on the ground by the White Owl. I took the folded paper out of my front pocket to look at the drawing once more. Looking closely at the sketch, I find myself

facing the same nightmare that my brother had once experienced. Overwhelmed by so much fear, I turn my head to look toward the horrific image standing before me. I cannot believe I am looking at a sketch of the same Dark Entity that haunted my brother just before his death.

OH MY GOD . . . , what does this Entity want with me?

Now, I must face the same Dark Entity that watches me from every corner of this pathway as I try to find a way out of this nightmare. I pray that the light coming from the candles stay lit as each one continues to flicker from the cold damp mist moving all around me. I watch the Entity continue to watch me as it hovers motionless from a distance. I am not sure what is about to happen with the White Owl standing between me and the Dark Entity, but the Dark Entity seems to refuse to come any closer. As horrifying and disturbing as this dark figure looks, its presence makes me believe I was purposely lured down this path to be led into its world. Suddenly, the White Owl turns its head toward my direction. It begins to change, becoming a bright, colorful light twisting and bending, causing me to look away. I squint trying to look but the image becomes too difficult to see. My eyes strain, trying to see what is happening in front of me. I rub my eyes to focus on what I am trying to look at, but they become irritated, causing dark spots to appear all around me. Something strange is continuing to happen as I try to shield my eyes to see what is happening in front of me. The White Owl begins to look blurry as it twists out of shape, waving back and forth, unlike anything I have ever experienced. I am so scared, especially knowing the Dark Entity is watching and waiting from a distance and I am unaware of its intentions. I turn away from the White Owl to keep myself from looking at this shapeless wavy image causing me to feel dizzy.

I can still smell the rancid stench in the air, letting me know the Entity is nearby. I needed to find out what was also on the drawing to see if there is anything else that might be able to help me. The drawing must have been given to me as a forewarning, a sign to keep me safe.

Looking at the paper still in my hand, I carefully look over the drawing while my vision begins to clear up from the effects of the White Owl. Apart from the shadow-like figures behind the Dark Entity, there is nothing different from what I saw before. But now looking closely at everything sketched on the paper, I see something above the dark figures at the top in the right-hand corner. I see a small sketch of a cross identical to the one I have inside my pocket. The same cross I nearly lost earlier when I took the cloth out of my pocket to wipe my eyes. Now I know how important the cross is, especially when my brother's spirit helped me find it after falling out of the cloth onto the ground. There are things David sketched on this paper that he saw manifesting from his nightmares. Somehow, David is trying to protect me from another place far away, just as he did when he was alive.

Looking up with my hands shielding my eyes from the distorted image of the White Owl, I carefully put the drawing back inside my pocket. I still see the Entity watching as it stays in place, surrounded by the mist swirling around its long pitch-black hair that moves like strands of black smoke emanating in and out of the darkness. I have never felt so much fear watching "something" truly horrifying as it hovers above the ground of this pathway. The Entity has stopped from coming any closer. The White Owl seems to be the only thing standing between me and the Dark Entity. At this moment, my biggest fear is being captured by that "thing" and trapped forever inside this nightmare . . .

CHAPTER 10

REALM OF THE WITCH

STILL SQUINTING, I try to see through this vivid image of what I thought to be the White Owl standing before me.

I rub my eyes, trying to focus on this image that is changing right in front of me. Suddenly . . . *Oh, my God* . . . I see the image start to take the form of a lady kneeling on the ground. Her head is facing downward so I cannot see her face. She is wearing a long white dress with sleeves covering her hands. She is totally silent, not saying anything. Her short hair covers half of her face.

Overwhelmed by so much fear, all I can do is watch the lady looking down toward the ground as if she were praying. I do not know whether to run or stand here and wait to see what she is going to do. At this moment, I am so frightened. I know she is the only one keeping the Dark Entity from getting any closer to me.

As the lady starts to stand up, she looks directly at me. I look at her and cannot believe what I see. I am shocked and confused at the same time, trying to understand what is going on. I take a couple of steps back while staring at the lady in disbelief. I just cannot believe how much she looks like my Aunt Vera, who recently passed away. She stands there looking at me, moving her head slightly side to side as if she is trying to figure out who I am. I am too frightened to say anything. I know deep down inside she can help me find my way back home. I cannot take my eyes off of her as I try to force myself to ask her so many questions, but nothing seems to come out of my mouth. I look past the lady and still see the Entity. I desperately force myself to ask who she is. She stands there without any kind of expression on her face, not saying anything. She only stares right at me.

I ask her again, "Who are you?" She starts to move slowly toward me, dragging her long white dress across the ground. I turn sideways, flinching, unsure of what she is going to do to me. She stops just in front of me and whispers, "Robert . . . you know who I am."

My voice begins to sound shaky as I nervously respond by saying, "You look like my Aunt Vera . . . is that who you are?"

(In a whispering voice) "Yes."

"This can't be true . . . my Aunt Vera is gone . . . you can't be !"

The lady says, "I was sent to you for protection from the Witch I once faced when I was living. She has come for you . . . to take you back into a world which lies deep inside this darkness, as she once tried with David. This "Dark Witch" wants your soul. I can help you . . . only when you have found what you have come here for."

"I don't understand . . . what do you mean?"

She bends down toward me and whispers, "I will always be with you. There are things along this path that will take you further away from who you are. Be aware of what hides deep inside this darkness while drawing you closer to a world that your brother had almost fallen into. Remember, Robert . . . I will protect you from the Dark Witch who placed a curse on you and your family."

I put my head down, trying to understand what she said. Even though I am confused and scared of what I have already faced, my greatest fear now is being trapped with a Witch that could potentially come for me at any time. I do not want to be left alone with something so terrifying, capable of keeping me from never returning home. My only hope now is listening to a spirit who claims to be my Aunt Vera.

Could this be true? Could this be the same person whom I have known my whole life has come back to protect me? Or was she already here? It seems as if Aunt Vera's soul was trapped inside the White Owl, who now follows me. I suddenly think about David; he must also be here. Somehow, when Aunt Vera was alive helping my parents free my brother's soul from the Entity that once haunted him, David must have ended up here. My parents and I thought that my Aunt Vera had freed my brother so that he could finally be laid to rest. Unfortunately, he must have ended up here, along with the other unsettling things that are hidden within this path.

I'm suddenly having thoughts about why I am here. If Aunt Vera and David are both no longer living and wandering about this path like me, why do I still feel alive? Or am I . . . ? I still ponder the question of whether this is only a nightmare or am I in a place where your soul wanders from not accepting death. I begin to feel so much anxiety questioning my existence. I should be home sleeping in my bed, getting up early to pick up a Christmas tree with my dad. Instead, I am in another place filled with spirits of my family and dark figures that haunt me. I only wish my brother were still alive today so I would not have to be here, stuck inside this dreadful place. *But, why . . . why was I led to this place? Why have I been taken from life to be here inside this nightmare?*

I thought about what the spirit of my Aunt Vera said, "I can help you, only when you have found what you have come here for." *What does she mean? I don't understand why I am even here.* I put my head down, just wanting to give up.

Feeling so hopeless, I am surrounded by darkness with no way out. Trapped inside a nightmare that never seems to end. A nightmare created by a curse placed upon me and my brother. A curse causing me to somehow fall into this dark world. My only hope of getting out of here is by trusting a White Owl claiming to be my Aunt Vera sent here to help. Unlike my Aunt Vera whose purpose is to protect me, what purpose does my brother have here with me? What is keeping him here? I saw my Aunt Vera help David's spirit be laid to rest two years ago. What has caused him to return to this cold, dark, and lonely place?

I lift my head and ask Aunt Vera's spirit, "Will the Dark Witch come for me if you leave?"

The spirit replies, "No."

Aunt Vera's spirit starts to walk back slowly as she continues to look at me. She kneels on the ground, becoming this bright, distorted, and blurry image, causing me to turn away as she begins to change right before my eyes. No sooner than I turn away, the White Owl appears again, standing where Aunt Vera's spirit had been kneeling. I look around, confused about where she went. Only the White Owl stands before me with its wings spread out, ready to take flight. I begin to get frightened again as I'm going to be left alone with the Witch that watches me from a distance. I look past the White Owl for the Dark Witch, and I no longer see it on the path. I know the Witch is still somewhere inside this darkness, just waiting for any chance to get me.

The White Owl now suddenly takes off, leaving me here standing alone and scared. I begin to slowly walk, hoping nothing else unsettling will appear from inside the dark walls along this path. Having already seen this Witch appear before me, I cannot keep from thinking that every noise or shadow from a flickering candle could be this scary creature lurking nearby in the dark and suddenly stepping out into the light. Keeping my eyes straight ahead, I begin to see this path as an endless passage into another world. Even though there are no actual walls on either side of me, the darkness becomes the walls, keeping me on this cold, dreary path. Darkness is too terrifying to enter without having any light to help find your way around. Nevertheless, my only choice is to keep watching out for the Dark Witch, among other unknown things that possibly stay within these illusional walls of darkness.

The stench still lingers in the air from the presence of the Dark Witch. The overwhelming smell of rotted mold has now weakened from the evil Entity that has disappeared into the darkness. Yet, still threatened by all the bad things hiding along this pathway, I cannot help from being scared as I keep wandering along this grim pathway, hoping for any sign of finding my way back.

Still guided by the flickering candles that stayed lit, I begin to hear rain falling all around me. I can smell the scent of lavender in the air once again. I stop to look all around as I turn in every direction to find out where all this is coming from. I hear rain falling all around me, but I do not feel any water hitting me. Something is happening . . . I start to remember the lavender flowers my mother always put on my brother's grave. Then, I remember the rain.

My mother held onto the lavender flowers until she placed them on my brother's casket just before he was lowered into the ground. She cried and cried and I sat close to her with my face pushed into her back to keep myself from looking at anyone. I cried with my mother as we watched my father help lower David to the ground. My father fell to his knees once he lowered the casket into the grave. He cried too for David as he grabbed a portion of dirt that was dug out next to the hole. He threw dirt into the grave with so much anger, asking why . . . why did this have to happen to my son?

I sat next to my mother, looking at the rain coming down all around us. We were under the cover that kept us from getting wet. Everyone stood close together, joining us under the cover to keep from becoming drenched. So much sadness filled the air. My parents and I watched every bit of dirt shoveled into the grave until David was completely covered.

I remember going home and putting my clothes away. I can still hear the rain coming down while looking at David's bed as it now stood empty. I stood next to his bed, still hearing the pain coming from Mom's weeping as she held onto her dying son. Those painful images uncontrollably still go through my head, even though I forced myself not to think about that tragic night. I walked over to the bedroom window to watch the rain come down. I opened the curtain and saw a lavender flower sitting on the windowsill. Surprised by what I saw, I knew this was a sign of his presence. At such a young age, I would have never thought this could be a cry for help or just letting me know that he was okay.

Clearing my mind, I had to focus on what is happening right now. The scent of the lavender becomes stronger, and the candles begin to flicker as a strange breeze goes by. I keep looking back, making sure nothing terrifying is behind me. Suddenly, I see someone sitting on the ground just ahead of me with their arms and legs crossed and their head down between their knees. I begin to slowly approach a little boy crying. I notice the boy is wearing brown corduroy pants and a sweater, so I know right away who he is. I said, "David . . . David . . . why are you crying?"

He sits there sobbing with his head down. I start to put my hand on his shoulder to comfort him and I catch a glimpse of a dark shadow just ahead, crossing over the path back into the darkness. I tell David to come with me, something is wrong . . . we need to get out of here. The sound of the rain stops and the smell of the lavender goes away. Everything around me becomes silent and the stench of rotted mold returns. David sits there sobbing and ignoring what I am telling him. I have no intention of leaving him behind, not knowing what might happen to him.

As he is still ignoring me, I yell for David as I watch this dark shadow-like figure begin to slowly move into the light. I desperately scream for David to come with me as more of those dark figures appear from the pitch-dark walls of the pathway. As the figures emerge from the darkness, I can see their terrifying faces appear partially visible in the dim light. I have never seen anything so horrifying as I stand next to David while screaming for him to get up and run. Each one resembling a monkey, grinning with so much evil coming from their face. Their large dark eyes stare directly at me as each one moves into the pathway. Their heads begin twitching erratically, rapidly moving side to side, becoming disfigured and too unsettling to look at. Suddenly, I hear a voice telling me to leave him alone. Again, I hear a voice say, "leave him alone."

I quickly turn around and see the spirit of Aunt Vera telling me to leave him alone.

"I'm trying to force my brother to leave with me."

Again, the spirit says, "Leave him there."

"I can't, they will get him . . . ," I yell.

"He is not your brother . . . the Dark Witch is trying to lure you into her realm. The other dark shadow-like figures are here to feed off your fears just like they did when David was going through his own terrifying nightmares . . . get away from him."

"But . . . I smell the lavender," I start screaming loudly at the spirit, "He is my brother, he is here with me."

"No, they are using your memories to lead you to their dark world," said Aunt Vera.

I stood up and backed away from the one I thought to be my brother. Suddenly, he lifts his head and looks directly at me. I threw myself back and saw something other than my brother looking at me. I saw an evil face that resembled those dark figures standing before me. He stares at me with the same evil grin as the others while laughing in a high-pitch, crackling voice. Aunt Vera's spirit told me to back away so they could go back where they came from. I continue looking at this evil monkey face I thought was David as it begins to stand up from the ground.

It turns to face the wall of darkness and quickly glances at me before disappearing back into its world. I looked at those hideous dark figures and saw that their heads had stopped moving. Their evil monkey faces watched me from a distance as they stood in place whispering over one another, sounding like an overlapping mass of prayers echoing all around me. Together, they intentionally try to devise a way to lead me into their ungodly path to devour my soul. I may fear those entities patiently waiting for me, but my fear lies more toward the evil Dark Witch who is near.

The spirit with her long white gown draped onto the ground says, "Follow me to get away from the dark figures, which have now started to haunt you. This dark world which you are in you have seen outside your bedroom window at night. You often wondered where the White Owl would go when it disappears into the night after leaving from the barn. It is this same dark world you find yourself trapped inside with all the things hidden all around you. Your brother was haunted by these same shadow-like figures that you have seen so far. Everything that happened to your brother has now started to happen to you.

"The curse that Uncle Eddie placed on you and your brother is to blame for all the bad things happening to you. David faced the same entities inside his nightmares that manifested from inside this dark world you have ended up in. This makes it easier for someone like Aunt Barbara to have kept track of David. By using her Black Magic in your world and not inside this dark pathway, where her power becomes too weak, she uses other entities to come and go through this pathway into your world. By Barbara being near your family she could feed off David's and your fear while strengthening the "evil" that hides within the darkness in the same world you and she share.

"Barbara created these dark figures to wait for your brother's soul until the curse was fulfilled by sending Uncle Eddie over to your house to cause the tragedy that still follows your family today. I may have helped your brother's soul leave your world from a curse placed by Barbara, but he is still stuck between both worlds causing you to still see him. You are here for a reason. You are too vulnerable to face this alone in your world. Barbara is much stronger in your world than inside this pathway. You were brought here to have a better chance to end this curse."

Looking at the spirit with so much to think about, I only had one question, "I thought you freed my brother's spirit after helping us rid of this evil Entity from inside our house."

"Unfortunately, by helping David become free and ridding the evil from your lives, instead, your brother's soul became lost. His spirit ended up here while the Entity I call the "Dark Witch" returned to its realm," said Aunt Vera.

"Yes, the Entity that haunted your brother . . . it is the Witch who now lives here . . . this is her realm. In the world you come from, you become vulnerable to the fears that grow inside your soul allowing the dark figures, hiding all around you at night, to become stronger. Your brother, who saw them at night, became vulnerable to the same shadow-like figures that are here with us now. Sadly, your brother succumbed to this curse, leaving behind so much pain for you and your parents. Your Aunt Barbara feeds off the dark energy that has manifested into an evil Dark Witch that follows you and your family today. You must stay here until you get what you came here for."

Aunt Vera's spirit slowly backs up and kneels to the ground. She starts to become this image once again, unbearable to look at as I try to get more answers to what she said. Her image begins to shape-shift into the White Owl, causing me to turn away. Feeling the frustration of what she told me, I start to get louder to get her attention while shielding my eyes, but she flies off, disappearing into the pathway. I continue yelling, "Wait . . . ! What did I come here for? . . . I don't understand!"

Repeatedly, I still hear the spirit of my Aunt Vera telling me that I cannot leave until I get what I came here for. I do not understand. I am so scared of what I must face coming from inside these dark boundaries that has made everything become so hopeless. I want to just give up. I just want to go home and be with my parents.

CHAPTER II
MONKEY FACES

I SEE THE DARK FIGURES still standing far behind me while their overlapping whispers start to fade as I walk farther away from those terrifying faces showing from inside the dim light.

I know . . . I saw those horrifying faces somewhere before. I just cannot remember where I saw those evil monkey faces behind me. I took the drawing out of my front pocket to look over the sketches again to see if I might have missed something on this paper. I look closely at the sketch of the dark shadows surrounding the Evil Witch. Nothing. I look at the cross on the top right-hand corner then I turn my attention back to the dark figures behind the Witch while carefully looking for anything that might help me.

Wait . . . the "Witch" is holding a long, skinny metal bar in her hand. I look more closely to what she is holding, and I see a round head attached to the bar. It looks like the head of a monkey. I look at the dark figures on this paper once more, but I cannot see their faces. Why do I see the monkey face on the bar and not on the dark figures in the drawing? David must have seen this bar with the evil monkey head held by the Dark Entity in his nightmares. What does this mean? Could it be another warning from David . . . ? I will never know, having to face the fear which renders only the assurance of being lost inside this dark world with so many unexplained things around me. The same dark world that has become a home to all the terrifying things hiding behind these pitch-dark walls that seem to feed off my fears, making me vulnerable to everything on this poorly lit path.

My Aunt Vera may be right. Barbara had used these entities to pass through this pathway into my world, forcing me to face all the same frightening things my brother once did. A pathway brought upon by Barbara only to cause so much fear and malice inside my life. The very same pathway used to conjure up those dark figures to appear in my nightmares before ending up with them inside this dark place. I can only watch in fear as they manifest and wait patiently inside this darkness to get me. I just hope that if I have to face the same fate as my brother, *Please GOD . . . don't let me be stuck inside this nightmare forever.* My fear begins to take over, causing me to panic and get these flashes of memories outside this dreadful place.

I am remembering how I would sit on the edge of an empty canal or hang around the pond near our house just outside the walnut orchard. During the winter, the canal and pond would become empty, leaving behind pieces of wood and dead shrubs sitting on top of the sand. I would walk through the walnut orchard to make my way to the canal. Once I stepped onto the dirt road that runs along the canal, I would walk until I reached the paved road to cross over the bridge to the other side of the canal to make my way to the pond, where I would spend my whole day looking for things on the sand.

Other days, I would just hang around the pond to get away from everything. Sometimes, there were moments I would sit down under the bridge of the canal to think about what was happening in our house each night as I tried to go to sleep. I knew something was not right living in this house. I was not alone at night when I would find myself sleepwalking in the back bedroom. It seemed like each night I would be drawn in by something living here inside the bedroom at the back of the house. I would feel as if someone were watching me as I stood standing alone in the dark, looking around without any recollection of how I got there.

Nevertheless, I would have to face each night trying to ignore the strange things going on all around me. Unfortunately, trying to avoid what was happening became more and more difficult to deal with. Especially not knowing who or what was lurking around inside our house late at night. Playing outside all day around the ranch would help me forget about what I was experiencing. I never stayed out too late when evening started to set in. Nothing was more frightening than what was waiting in the dark surrounding our house when daylight disappeared. The many big walnut trees surrounding our house seemed to block out any moonlight.

All of our relatives already knew about this house, often telling us stories about the strange things that took place here long before we moved in. Whether the stories were just fabricated or real, my *own* fear was REAL. It came from the real things that started to happen after my dad came back from visiting Aunt Barbara to seek out answers to why Uncle Eddie did what he did. Later, we found ourselves facing something horrifying that had attached itself to the family. We were unaware of David's presence also following us from the one-bedroom house in town after his tragic death. David's spirit crossed into the path of this Dark Entity that moved around inside this house. Aunt Barbara attached something evil to my father the night he went to see her, almost costing David's soul to be taken away by this Dark Entity—the one I believe is the Dark Witch. This curse placed onto me and my brother by Barbara has taken away our peace.

Before finding the reason behind the strange things that were happening to me and my family, we were still carrying the enormous pain of losing my brother. My parents never gave a second thought about David's spirit attaching itself to this family or having to face anything from beyond. We only knew about the curse for one of us to die in seven years. We never thought that our lives would revolve around this dark world. Aunt Barbara never told my father why she sent Uncle Eddie to our house that night. She does not seem to think that my brother's death caused enough pain by attaching these dark entities and evil witches to my family. Seems so unfair that this person who is supposed to be part of our family would create such a world to feed into her own selfish intentions. And never giving any sign of remorse for what she had done to all of us.

Walking into this house on the ranch for the first time was supposed to be a change for me and my parents. I had no idea what was about to happen. Then, the night sets in and the darkness unleashes all the bad things hidden in every corner of our house. Every dark figure and shadow appearing from out of the dark becomes unavoidable, causing me to feel the fear that makes those ungodly spirits become stronger. They seem to feed off my fear as well as my anxiety causing me to become terrified of what the night and darkness would bring.

Unaware of what was happening inside our new house, I tried to ignore these strange occurrences at night. I tried everything to avoid waking up in the middle of the night, like staying up later so I would sleep without waking up until it was time for me to get up for school. Unfortunately, I still found myself waking up close to three in the morning confronted by the unsettling images manifesting all around me.

During the day, I would spend my time outside just to get away from all the things that were happening to me inside our house. But then there were times when I left my house that I felt as if I was being followed, especially when I would run home through the orchard at night hearing noises coming from all around me. I would look around, scared, hoping not to see anything hiding behind those walnut trees. I would often think about David and wonder if he was the one following me. I guess I still felt sad at not having my brother here with me.

My emotions always seem to change. Going from being that normal kid during the day then having to face the strange things happening at night, while feeling sad about not having my brother around. But nothing could have prepared me and my parents for what Aunt Vera would have to tell us after spending a couple of days with us. She had found herself awakened by an apparition of a small child inside her mobile home late at night parked in our backyard. She told my mother what she saw that same night but found it difficult to tell us that the apparition was actually David's spirit. She feared that my mother would become upset. After leaving our house without saying too much, she gave it more thought and felt she needed to tell my parents the truth. She telephoned them and said she would be paying them another visit because she needed to tell them something important.

When Aunt Vera returned to our house the next day, she explained everything to us. My parents believed everything she said since they knew her life revolved around the supernatural world and the practice of her "White Magic." Even though everything started to make sense when she told us about David's spirit visiting her, I became even more scared when she told us there was an evil presence also residing inside *our* home.

I knew then that the strange things happening at night must have been David. Or was it someone—or something—else? I found it difficult to distinguish one from the other—the occurrences from my brother's spirit or the Dark Entity. The only indication that would confirm the presence of the evil presence was the rotted stench I could smell at certain times during the night. Before I ever knew about what Aunt Vera had experienced at our house, I was already suffering anxiety from unexpected things happening to me during the night.

Sleepwalking became a nightly occurrence. I often find myself waking up inside the back bedroom, standing in front of the window that faces out toward the old barn. Standing alone in the dark and wondering how I got here, I hear noises coming from inside the bedroom. Like . . . a strange knocking coming from the wall behind the empty bed. This knocking is not the only time this has occurred. When we lived in the house in town, David too often heard knocking going across the wall above his bed late at night. Now I am beginning to remember these same things happening to my brother. Why am I hearing the same knocking when I wake up in the middle of sleepwalking and find myself inside the back bedroom? Am I going to end up like David?

The only thing that has made my nightmares different from what my brother went through is that I am not alone. I have David giving me these signs from the "other side" to help me get through this dreadful place that I have been dragged into. I can now see the signs left behind by David, whereas before, when he was alive, I never saw the signs of what David was experiencing when he would draw these dark figures on a piece of paper. I just stood by and watched everything bad happening to him. Now I am left with this heavy burden inside me from not realizing what he was going through.

I now watch these same dark figures with their evil monkey faces watching from a distance. I have a sudden, unexpected memory of seeing one of those dark figures appear over David just before his life ended. I can sense how it was draining his soul up until his sudden death. I cannot stop seeing his eyes when he looked at me from our mother's arms as life had already drained out of him. Standing at the foot of his bed and watching in horror, I will never forget how he looked at me with those eyes wide open and empty. I am left with the nightmares of what I saw that night along with these dark figures that still haunt me.

Ending up here in a place that keeps this constant fear of not knowing what is going to happen next has kept me from realizing other things happening around me. As a result, I realize that David's spirit has been trying to help me with his drawings since becoming lost here. As I find myself becoming more lost inside this dark world, I am drawn closer to where my brother has ended up. A world where the images have become stranger and more surreal. Like the things that appear from inside this pathway.

Now, not only do I have to face an evil Dark Witch inside this dreadful nightmare, I must also be confronted by all the dark figures that are led by her malice only to cause harm to me. The dark figures with their large evil smirks seem to manifest from where this dark, cold, and terrifying Dark Witch comes from. A darkness she has created releasing the evil entities which descend from a world hidden deep within her realm, plaguing the night with all its negative energy. A world that opens when the night falls, causing the darkness to become a pathway connection between both worlds.

Somehow, Barbara is responsible for creating this pathway to use the Dark Entities for her selfish evil intent. She created the Dark Entities to use her Black Magic coming for me as she tried with my brother. Barely saved from the clutches of this evil Witch, my Aunt Vera was unable to help him completely to be laid to rest. Somehow David's soul and spirit became separated, lost between both worlds two years ago when Aunt Vera stopped the evil entity (Dark Witch) from dragging him into the darkness forever. Unfortunately, Aunt Vera can no longer help my brother since she is now dead, but her spirit has somehow passed through this pathway shape-shifting into the White Owl. With her spirit bound to this creature that protects me within this pathway, she can still help me and my brother find our way home.

The dark, evil witch is reflected in Barbara along with every bad thing that hides inside her dark world—a world made up of an empty, cold, pitch-black hole infested with Dark Entities used to carry pain and suffering into our lives. These Entities hidden in the dark with their evil faces resembling that of a monkey inflict so much fear on me that they push me further into a terrifying endless path. These faces of evil, partially hidden as they smile from a distance, mimics each other with overlapping whispers heard along the path. Their evil sounds leave behind constant echoes that stay inside my head to purposely place fear inside me.

Standing on this path barely realizing the drawing was still in my hand, I have placed it back into my front pocket. I notice everything around me has become quiet. I turn from one side to the other looking for those dark figures that seem to have disappeared along with their evil whispers echoing throughout the pathway. One thing that did not make any sense was the sketch of the evil monkey head attached to the skinny metal bar resembling each of the dark figures watching me from inside these pitch-dark walls surrounding me. Somehow, the images of those faces have become much more than a nightmare. Images that have become real and lifelike, pulling me away from the real world.

I continue to walk aimlessly without any guidance from the spirits of my Aunt Vera or David. I feel lost and unaware of my purpose for being here. Afraid of never finding my way back, thoughts go through my mind imagining that I will be forced to live forever inside this darkness and never know if I am still alive or dead, lost between two worlds. I believe being alive and lost in a dark world is much worse than being dead, because I would be confronted by every thought and emotion of living inside this darkness. Whereas death takes away the soul, which contains who you are, leaving behind an emotionless, unrested spirit. Still having all my emotions with me now, my life here inside this nightmare has become a terrifying journey into an endless world of dark emptiness.

Nevertheless, I still feel very much alive . . . searching for a way out back to my world. I still fear the evil lurking all around me, and I stand defenseless and alone while hoping not to see the evil entity and the dark figures ever again. The fear of being confronted by the horror that hides along this dark path overwhelms me with so much anxiety as

I wait for something too dreadful to appear. I can sense a presence all around me, but I will have to get through this nightmare by doing what the spirit of Aunt Vera told me—find what I came here for.

I cannot help being so scared of what I will see as I start walking along this poorly lit path of burning candles. These candles are the only light giving me a sense of hope, a chance to return home and wake up in the morning to help my father find a Christmas tree. So far, it is unlikely that I will ever go home.

CHAPTER 12
THE TRANSIENT

MY ARMS ARE CROSSED, pulled up to my chin as I desperately try to keep myself warm. I keep looking around for any signs of finding my way out of here.

A breeze goes right past me as I watch the candles start to flicker along the path. Suddenly, I smell lavender once again, just like before when I saw the little boy standing next to Dr. Scott. I quickly start looking around to see if the little boy is nearby. Nothing . . . the lavender still lingers all around me. I stand completely still to listen or notice anything strange causing the candles to flicker. My body begins to shake uncontrollably from the cold breeze hitting me as it moves along the path, almost blowing out the flames of the spirit candles which are guiding me through the darkness.

At this moment, my fear has completely taken over. Panic has already set in as I turn frantically back and forth in each direction. My anxiety gets worse while I wait for something unexpected to happen. So terrified . . . hoping and praying that nothing dreadful is going to appear from within the darkness that runs along this pathway—a darkness, unlike the darkness that surrounds me at night when I am sleeping. A darkness created from a hidden world made up of invisible boundaries used to hide all the Dark Entities that appear inside this nightmare.

Unfortunately, the nightmare is more of a world that was placed upon me than a nightmare created inside my head. Whether this experience is real or just a bad dream . . . I'm scared. This nightmare has become more a struggle to keep my Soul than to find my way back from being lost between both worlds. With all that has happened so far along this path, I am beginning to think that I am a connection to a dark force from the past that has brought me here for some purpose. Despite what I believe, I remain with the faces of evil which are waiting for any chance to appear and drag me into their dark realm.

Suddenly, without warning, something tugs on my shirt behind me. I quickly turn around. I see a little boy standing in front of me while I feel a strange coldness hit my face. I quickly jump back, falling to the ground, startled from the image standing motionless while a chill runs through my body as if he has been carried by the cold breeze that moved along this path. I call out David's name . . . unsure if I am looking at my brother or someone else. I have to believe the spirit standing right in front of me is my brother. "David . . . it's your brother, Robert."

The little boy stands with his head down, making it difficult for me to see his face. He slowly lifts his head up, looking directly at me without any kind of expression showing on his face. I sense that this spirit is not evil, but still something seems different about the little boy. David's spirit was more vivid when he appeared to me, whereas this spirit looks dark and ghostly. Uncertain if this presence is my brother's spirit, he still resembles a little boy who seems harmless. The spirit stares at me motionless without any reaction or feelings. He stands before me with a shadow covering part of his face. I look around while feeling concerned about his presence. I am confused as to why this spirit seems different. Different in such a way that I sense an empty, cold loneliness coming from this little boy. I continue to watch the spirit of this little boy who seems more like a soul lost in transience from another time and place. An unfamiliar presence bound by a tragedy, intentionally led here by the same entities that have led me into an endless path of nothing. I feel no connection coming from this spirit, unlike the connection I have felt with my brother's spirit. Obviously this spirit is connecting with me for a reason that I have yet to understand.

Suddenly, I'm thinking about the image of the little boy who stood next to Dr. Scott pointing into the darkness just before I was given David's drawing earlier into this nightmare. Even though I can smell the lavender scent still in the air, the smell allows me to believe that David is nearby. If the spirit is not David, why do I smell the lavender lingering in the air?

Looking around and still feeling so frustrated and scared, I call out, "Where are you, David? . . . Where are you?"

Then I look back at the spirit, "Who are you . . . if you're not my brother?"

The spirit moves toward me and takes my hand to follow him. I get up off the ground to find out where this little boy is leading me. He stops and stares straight ahead, pointing into the empty pathway. He is pointing in the direction where he wants me to continue walking. He stands with his head facing toward the ground as if he is not allowed to go any farther. I look at him for a moment, wondering who or why he is here with me. Again, I ask, "Who are you?"

Still no response. I become hesitant, afraid of what I will see if I continue to walk where the spirit of the little boy has so far led me. I force myself to continue to keep walking while looking over my shoulder, watching the little boy still standing behind me.

I start to hear strange noises just ahead. Unfamiliar voices . . . not the voices I have heard echoing from those dark figures. But voices of a man and woman talking over one another. Suddenly, I begin to hear the lady's voice sound frightened as she seems to plead with the man who sounds angry. I walk toward the voices to find out who these people are. All I can see are two shadows starting to become vivid as I get closer to the voices. I can hear the man's voice get louder as the woman starts to cry, still pleading with the man. I can see the dark figures become clear as I see a man appear dressed in a long-sleeve shirt with baggy brown slacks. He is wearing a fedora hat that looks like the hat my grandfather used to wear. The woman crying is wearing a long yellow dress with flowers. Her long black curly hair is pinned up on both sides of her head. They look like people from the old movies my father watches on television. I feel so sad watching that woman crying. I do not know why the spirit of the little boy wants me to see this. Feeling confused, I turn around to see if the little boy is still standing behind me. Out of nowhere, I see Dr. Scott standing next to the little boy as they both watch me. I turn back quickly to find the man and woman gone. I am so confused to why I am seeing the image of the man fighting with the woman. I do not understand why the little boy has shown me an image of those people that I have never seen before. *Where is my brother's spirit? I can smell the lavender all around me . . . I know he is here with me . . . I really need him here right now.*

I feel so alone and confused. I feel so scared. Why I am stuck here in a place that makes me feel that I'm already dead? Already taken from my parents. Never having a chance to grow up, feeling sad Never . . . having a chance to pick out a Christmas tree with my father in the morning before ending up inside this nightmare.

I have experienced so much with all that I have faced being here. I have yet to understand anything about the entities and the dark figures who seem to appear in a place which has become a sense of reality instead of a nightmare. Unclear if fate has deliberately drawn me into this place driven by those who have watched me sleep at night, I fear that the curse placed on me and my brother by Aunt Barbara has created unexplained occurrences connecting to my brother's death, and me ending up here. Yet, I stand here inside this dim, dreary place watching the image of a little boy and Dr. Scott, who seems to be a part of this dark world forced upon me without any reason. The connection between the little boy and Dr. Scott has little to do with what I have been experiencing with the Entity and the dark figures that hide behind those evil faces.

Suddenly, I remember what Dr. Scott told me about not holding onto things too long because I will eventually surround myself with 'really' scary stuff that will keep me from being happy.

Could Dr. Scott be here because of those scary things that he was trying to warn me about? Is that why he is here? A warning for me to let go of everything that I have so far experienced from a tragedy during a vulnerable time of my life, a life that I have barely begun? I stand here looking at the spirit of the little boy along with Dr. Scott as they watch me. Both standing lifeless as their images become transparent, like two ghostly figures without any kind of emotion or any reason of why they are here.

The smell of lavender becomes stronger. I quickly start turning and circling around looking for any signs of my brother's spirit nearby. I can only see the little boy and Dr. Scott still standing alongside the path watching me. I start to panic and all I can see are the spirit candles placed along the ground, creating an opening of flickering dim lights fading off into the complete darkness.

I still wonder who intentionally placed these candles, creating this pathway that seems to go on forever as each flame never seems to burn out. Looking in both directions, a sadness comes over me and I get a pain inside my stomach, causing me to bend over with my hands over my knees. I feel like I need to vomit as I look back and forth, watching the image of the little boy standing next to Dr. Scott.

I turn away to look in the direction where I am going to start walking and suddenly I see the lady in the white dress appear with another little boy standing next to *her*. I look back toward the image of Dr. Scott and still see the little boy standing next to him. I stand up and know I am looking at my brother's spirit next to the lady in the white dress who is the spirit of Aunt Vera. Again, I turn back to look at the little boy with Dr. Scott and they are no longer there.

Feeling so confused about seeing another little boy's spirit, I turn to walk toward Aunt Vera to find out who the other little boy was standing next to Dr. Scott. Both Aunt Vera and David's spirit start to walk backwards, gradually disappearing into the pitch-dark walls, and the lavender scent starts to dissipate, leaving behind a smell of aging dust. I just stare into the darkness where Aunt Vera and David disappeared, wondering what to do next.

Overwhelmed by this endless nightmare, once again I am left searching for hope. Each terrifying experience is followed by another, leading me into nowhere. The light within this place has given me direction without any guidance. Could this be what death is like when you are lost?

My mother used to say, *"The White Owl senses death of a lost soul."* She would continue to tell me about the White Owl sitting on top of our house at night, attaching itself to a soul trapped between two worlds. As much as I try not to think about being one of those lost souls, I cannot help but wonder if I *am* indeed trapped, searching for the *very* same world I was taken from. *Can I be too late . . . ?*

I *am* trying to find my way out of here, when, in fact, there seems to be no hope of ever leaving this place. Over and over, the same thoughts continue to make everything hopeless. Confused and angry, I start to blame God as to why I am here. So many emotions go through my mind, yet I stand here and still ask God to help me.

Watching the little boy next to Dr. Scott reappear and disappear makes me believe that something else is happening. Something or someone has led this spirit into this nightmare. Unlikely pulled in by a coincidence, but somehow connected through a path led by the same things that have already taken hold of me. I am bound by this darkness which has placed so much burden inside me along with a sadness that instills the pain that never seems to go away. All the memories of the people who have been a part of my life one way or another have come back to help me up to this point, unscathed by all the bad things hidden within this darkness.

Although so far I have been kept from harm's way, I can feel my anxiety is gradually being replaced by a numbness that continues to grow inside me. I stand here trapped inside a world driven by unanswered questions with my every moment searching for something that I do not understand. I remain lost without any guidance, forced to wait for something else terrifying to happen. Wandering aimlessly disconnected from a world I may never return to. The only way to get through all of this is by becoming emotionally numb inside in order to make this nightmare less difficult to cope with as *hope* starts to fade. No matter how much I force myself to feel, something pulls me right back on this same path that I am desperately trying to get away from. I just become more confused and feel more trapped without ever having any answers to what is going on. Just when I thought I found my answer to one question, something else arises, pushing me further away from why I am here.

Meaning, I was forced here to look for something that I have not found yet so that I can leave this place. Then . . . suddenly, out of nowhere, I now see someone else appear inside this nightmare, unaware who or where he has come from. Somehow, he is connected by a strange force, leaving behind another question that I am unable to answer. Possibly, this is prolonging my stay here inside this ungodly place. *Who is this little boy? And why did he show me the image of the man yelling at the woman?*

Watching other images from other people appear unexpectedly terrifies me, knowing that I might be here in this dark place to help bridge a gap between the souls that have become transients between two worlds as they pass through to the next life. I may be here for a purpose, a purpose which will keep me here forever within these dark walls that I am forced to wander.

Nevertheless, I must remain with the hope of getting home. Leaving this nightmare and finding my way back to the things I used to enjoy. Like running free around the walnut orchard, sitting quietly by the pond while listening to all the noises coming from the small animals around me, or just having normal nightmares that I can wake up from.

CHAPTER 13

TRAVELING SOUL

REFLECTING BACK AS I watch the water ripple across the pond while sitting on the embankment, I am thinking how lonely it feels out here.

I can see the sun start to slowly appear brighter as the morning brings out all the life that wanders freely all around me. Being alone has never bothered me, having been the only child now for the last four years. I have always felt as if I was waiting for my brother to walk into the house so I can overwhelm him with a million questions. I guess, in a way, Hope never allows me to be lonely. Often, I find myself withdrawn from others around me. I see the world differently, in such a way that I have kept myself from making any friends in school. My life just seems to revolve around David, along with the memories we shared together.

Every day I think about him, especially living on the ranch with no one my age living nearby. I do not feel David is actually gone forever, even though I may never see him again. I see our existence in a different way. I think we become reborn each time our life has ended, and our soul waits for us until we arrive to the next life in a different time and place. I never accepted that life is gone forever, and that our soul disappears into the darkness. I refuse to think that someone would never have any chance to begin a new life after using up his or her old one. That is why I believe my brother will come back in a different time and place. Whether I believe this to be true or not, nothing in this world will ever take away the hope of David and I becoming a family again one day.

David gone forever . . . is something that I cannot force myself to believe. In a strange way, I have created this world to keep everyone out because of not understanding me. Being alone allows me to think about all the memories when my family and I were all together. Like the moments when I would walk to the pond just to sit and think. I have always felt a sense of peace hanging around there, just remembering how things were between me and my brother. Sometimes I would think about how my life would have been if David were here today. Nevertheless, I sit alone thinking about how my life so far has become difficult to face, especially when something bad or strange occurs—which seems to happen all too frequently.

Sometimes, I think an unknown negative energy has been drawn to my family, causing so many unfortunate events leading up to this life that I am now facing. I guess the things that I have gone through with my parents have always been difficult to cope with, a life filled with tragedy and struggle. Then, I face the darkness at night coping with an evil energy which seems to have attached itself to me and my parents, bringing out those Dark Entities that feed off my fear and the pain that I have gone through from a life I have just begun.

My life simply revolves around the way I see things and how I distinguish reality from a mysterious world which opens when I am alone, lying in bed terrified of what I must face during the night. Unfortunately, I wake up in the morning after a sleepless night only to be confronted by a world I must face every day as I try to understand why I see things the way I do through my eyes. A life filled with memories that simply disappear only to be replaced by others each time we move on to another life. Something inside has forced me to believe we live life after life with memories that fade as we travel into the next one.

I have looked out this window to the outside world every day, watching people staring back at me. I have often wondered if people can see what I see. If I am the only one that actually sees life become endless after we die. Endless in a way that we are given one life after another, each time we leave the next life. Meeting new family members along the way, only to never see them again once our time has ended. Is this what we look forward to after we use up our life, whether it is from old age or a tragic event? So many questions, yet too young to understand. I can only imagine my soul becoming faceless as I travel from one life to another.

Filled with sadness near the end, but every emotion seems to disappear going into the next life without remembering the one before. I have always seemed to end up scaring myself as I think about these things when I sit quietly alone watching the water from the pond hit against the embankment.

One early morning, I watched the tall grass sway along the pond from the morning breeze, and I breathed in the air through my nose, feeling the coldness as it started to fill my chest. I could not smell anything other than the algae coming from the water. The pond was starting to dry out from the sun and the tall grass had already grown above the water. Soon, all the animals that rely on the pond for food will be gone. Without any warning, everything that lives here now will die or disappear until next year. Life seems so short for the things that live here. I guess my life is not so bad. Every moment I sit here, my mind circles around the thought of wanting to be free from all the bad things that have been a part of me so far. I have always felt like a traveler, moving around with my family, and never having a real place I call home.

After moving out to the ranch, I still felt empty inside, alone even though I had my parents. I have always known that my father felt a sense of guilt for us having to get up and move from one home to another. Moving around had become normal for me and my family. Pop's drinking problem has always been an issue, with him losing job after job due to his drinking problem. Moving more often than I wanted to always gave me something to look forward to, I guess. But leaving behind my brother's memory was something that became exceedingly difficult to cope with. Moving around created this idea that I was a traveler; like the traveler I often think about when I must leave this life to wake up to another. But then I think about David. Nothing makes me sadder than never seeing my brother again as he travels until finding his other life.

I met my brother in this life for a short while, but I will have to live with knowing who he was. Nothing is forever, like the things that live inside this pond. I will never understand, only wonder if I will continue to travel in this life or the life which sits deep inside the darkness connected by all the memories that I have collected. Maybe . . . all the memories will become a story that will follow me to the next life. Stories which have been created only to be carried with me forever on an endless journey from one life into another, leaving behind all those who have cared for me. Like an endless traveler bound by fear, sadness, and pain. A traveler confined emotionally by the fear of being alone without any direction as I face the "unexpected."

I have already started to travel this journey without the only person who used to tell me that everything would be okay when something bad happened. I always felt safe with David when he was around. Now, I am forced to go through this world alone having to face the surreal images that haunt me. Over and over, I am overwhelmed by so many thoughts sitting alone watching every animal and insect around me continue to do what is needed to live here at this pond. I stare off in every direction listening for a voice to tell me that everything is going to be okay.

Unfortunately, only the silence surrounds me, and I am unable to keep myself from crying. Suddenly, I wipe my tears away with the back of my hands as I start laughing, feeling ridiculous hearing myself cry when everything around me remains calm. *See, nobody cares . . . nobody.*

Feeling frustrated and sad at the same moment, I got up off the ground and noticed someone under the bridge of the canal staring at me. I walked over toward the bridge and saw this person who looked like a small boy run out from under the bridge into the walnut orchard. I had to walk back onto the road to cross over the bridge to get to the other side to follow him. I could see him running with a gun that looked just like my BB gun I had sitting inside the corner of my closet. I chased him through the orchard, but he disappeared into the trees. I had never seen other kids around here before, especially since we had the only house on this road. I gave up looking for him and decided to just go home.

I walked into the house and saw my mother in the kitchen. I walked into my bedroom, and after shutting the door behind me, I sat on my bed. I looked toward my closet for a while, just staring at the door. As strange as everything was, I could not get myself to go into the closet. I was afraid of what I was going to find. Experiencing things at night was terrifying but seeing things during the day is worse because of the images that seem so real, like the people I see walking around during the day. It is not like the world that is created from the darkness where nightmares manifest these images that seem to come out only at night.

Having to distinguish the world I live in from a world made up inside my head becomes more difficult to understand; especially if I start to experience things that are not there *really* during the day. I needed to look inside my closet to make sure I wasn't going crazy. Slowly, I got up off my bed and walked up to the closet. I stood in front of the door, hesitating to look inside. Turning the doorknob slowly, I began to open the door while feeling my stomach start to hurt from the anxiety of what

I was going to see. The closet was very dark, making it difficult to see anything inside until the door was wide open to allow the light from my bedroom to shine in. I opened the door very slowly, standing as far away as I could from what might be inside.

Once I opened the door all the way, I was relieved not to see anything inside my closet. I started to push my clothes to one side to find my BB gun. I suddenly threw myself back landing on my butt just outside the closet while quickly pushing the door shut with my foot. I could not believe what I just saw! I sat on the floor staring at the closet door, becoming so terrified.

As I pushed the clothes to one side to look for my BB gun, I saw a small boy sitting in the corner of my closet holding my BB gun. He looked directly at me just inches away from my face, causing me to become horrified. I could not believe that this was the same little boy I saw running from under the bridge. Somehow, I knew we had this strange connection between us when I saw him. This is why I *knew* something was going to be inside my closet. I could not get myself to go back into the closet for quite a while. I knew deep down I was not crazy. But I also knew by seeing that image inside my closet that I was not alone like I thought I was.

Today, as terrifying as this may seem, my life began to become more complicated with unexpected images and fears that would soon take over and force me to end up inside this dreadful place. I am just like a traveler lost in time pulled into a faraway place only seen by the afterlife. I have started to experience things that unexpectedly appear during the day, not just at night. I have yet to understand why I stand here waiting, not knowing what my reason for being here is. Being emotionally drained by fear and anxiety makes me believe that I am alive and not a soul lost inside this darkness. Whether or not I was put here for a strange purpose, I am still a traveler caught up in a nightmare searching for answers.

CHAPTER 14

THE FORTHCOMING

THE IMAGES HAVE DISAPPEARED, so I have no choice but to continue walking farther along this boundless path.

I carefully follow the burning lights which flicker as each flame creates its own "shadow-like" figure along the ground behind me. Distracted by the distorted shadows appearing in the corner of my eyes, I begin to get closer and closer to the spirit candles, suddenly kicking one over. The candle slowly burns out as I look around waiting for something to happen. Fear comes over me while feeling upset that I have to experience all the terrifying things appearing within this dreadful dark place. Feeling scared and frustrated at the same moment, I begin to think how evil the dark figures hiding behind the burning candles seem; so cruel in wanting to intentionally hurt me while placing so much fear inside me. Perhaps it is possible that they want to draw me closer to them and further away from my world. *Well, I don't deserve to be here. I don't deserve to be punished as if I have done something so bad.*

I try to keep myself calm, constantly looking for any answers or signs leading me back to the only life that I have been taken from. Suddenly,

I'm thinking about what lies inside the darkness just beyond the spirit candles that were purposely placed along the ground on each side of me. I may never find out who intentionally placed each of those candles to create a path which seems to go on forever, but I need to know what lies inside the darkness that runs along behind the burning candles. Feeling so nervous and scared, I force myself to stop and turn my face toward this wall of darkness. I stand there for a moment, worried . . . scared of what I will see waiting for me inside. I slowly begin to walk over the candles, clutching my fist. I carefully stick my head into the pitch-black world that hides the Evil Witch and the dark figures who have tormented me and my family for much too long.

I continue to look around trying to see anything inside this complete darkness. I begin to breathe in an old musty mildew stench as my face starts to become cold. While bent over with my face still inside this complete darkness, I hear something behind me. I turn back to look over my shoulder from inside this dark place and see a large disfigured black shadow behind me in the corner of my eye. I quickly pull my head out into the light, and nothing is there. The shadow looked a little foggy from where I saw it, making it difficult to know what it was. I turn back from where I just pulled my head out of the wall of darkness and notice a strange mist starting to flow out. I quickly stick my head back in and my face immediately begins to get very cold. A nasty stench of rotten mold becomes overwhelming, forcing me to pull my head back out. I begin to feel scared, knowing that I have experienced the cold mist and the same rotted, moldy stench once before when the Witch appeared to me from a distance. I back away from the mist as it flows out into the light. The candles start to flicker. A humming noise is coming from inside my head causing me to have a bad headache.

I don't know what is happening. I back up farther away from the mist as it continues flowing out onto the path. Frantically, I turn around to run, trying to get far away from what is about to come out. The humming noise starts to turn into voices echoing inside my head, making it difficult to run straight. All I can think about is having no way to protect myself from what I believe to be the Witch who has no intention of leaving me alone. Falling to the ground from echoes inside my head, I quickly turn to see how far I have gotten, and a black mass starts to come out from the darkness while the mist becomes thicker, spreading more through the path.

The echoes in my head get louder and louder . . . my vision begins to become blurry. Difficult as it may seem to try to focus, I try to get up. I am horrified looking at the black mass moving into the light, unaware of what it is going to do to me. The echoes remain inside my head while my vision barely allows me to see what is now standing before me. Again, I see the dark image moving in a slow, back-and-forth, twisting motion. I see her thin translucent waves of black smoke expelling from her black translucent gown as it hovers closer to me. I see the long black strands of hair waving into the air, floating straight up above her shoulders. She is the most horrifying thing I have ever seen up close in the short time that I have been here. Worse than any nightmare I have ever had, her partially covered face is centered inside two rings of mist rotating in opposite directions.

Something is different this time from the last time this awful lady appeared to me. This time, the Dark Witch is closer, holding a round fiery ball in her hand as she looks toward me with her face partially covered by the darkness, resembling that of death. I do not know what to do without the help of Aunt Vera's spirit here to protect me. I am shaking so bad, terrified of what is about to happen. I finally get up off the ground and try to stagger away. I feel as if I am being held—somehow unable to escape from this horrifying evil Entity. Just like the nights when I find myself running from the dark figures inside my nightmares when I am asleep in my bed. Unfortunately, this nightmare is real, and I have no way of waking up. I start to scream for help, *I don't want to die . . . I don't want to die . . . Please GOD, help me.*

I scream and scream from the top of my lungs hoping for the Witch to go away. I can see her large black eyes start to appear. It is as if the Dark Witch knows that I have become vulnerable to her presence, making it much easier to take possession of my soul. I have become so numb inside from so much fear I cry and plead for help. I do not want to be stuck inside this darkness forever, unaware of what I will have to endure for eternity; never having had a chance to live out my life.

The candles begin to flicker in front of me. I look back and notice the Dark Witch moving closer and closer. The voices echoing inside my head are gone while the sounds of whispers begin to overlap one another throughout this path. Without warning, the dark figures of those partially covered monkey faces are now standing in front of me. Now I realize those horrible sounding whispers are coming from them. I look behind me and still see the Witch making her way toward me. I look in front of me again and see the dark figures standing on the path—waiting. Terrified at not having any way to escape, I kneel to the ground and start vomiting as I am now giving up. I look in each direction with my head facing the ground, vomiting uncontrollably. Soon, I feel a chill run through my body and feel something touching the top of my head. I slowly lift my head with tears running down the sides of my face ready to surrender with nowhere to go, when I suddenly see the lady with the white dress looking down at me.

I whispered, "Aunt Vera . . . you have come to save me."

She began to smile, "You know I will never let anything hurt you."

"But . . . the dark figures . . . the Witch. I have no way to pass them."

"You are safe with me, Robert," said the spirit.

"I can't find what I am supposed to look for like you asked me to do . . . I just want to go home."

"You cannot go home," said the spirit.

"Why?

"You have awakened, Robert, in the middle of a nightmare as you were watching yourself sleep. She . . . kept your spirit from returning to your body."

"But you said I woke up . . . I should be home in bed, not here."

"No . . . You woke up here. You are unable to go back into your body."

Confused by what the spirit of Aunt Vera is telling me, I ask, "How is this possible?"

"She waited until your spirit had been separated from your body, stopping you from returning by appearing inside your nightmare with you. As you became disembodied, she pulled you into this nightmare to complete her quest as she *almost* did with your brother. She cannot completely take total control of you, unless you become so lost that you cannot communicate with the spirits which still appear inside this path to protect you from Barbara's entities that she had created to take your spirit *and* soul."

"But David died by the hands of Uncle Eddie, not this lady you speak of."

The Aunt Vera spirit quietly explained, "You see, Robert, your Aunt Barbara had used her witchcraft to send those dark figures to your brother David to draw him into the same nightmare that you have ended up in. When David resisted, she sent Uncle Eddie to your house to place a curse on him. Eddie had pushed the front door in and confronted your parents in bed, which led to a struggle between him and your father, causing David's death. You see, Robert . . . the more she commits this evil, the more powerful her world becomes. For this, you must find what you have come here for."

"But . . . but . . . for what have I come here? I don't understand . . . has Barbara already taken my brother's soul? That is why I see his spirit here?"

"No, if she takes control of you, she will also have the power to take David's soul as well. With you here, you may have a chance to save yourself and your brother. That is why you are here. Find what is needed to leave this place and save your brother before it is too late."

With her long white dress flaring out along the ground, she gradually moves back as a light appears near both of her hands. Her long sleeves, which hang over each hand, make it difficult to see what she is holding. She gradually lifts both of her arms straight out, pointing the lights in each direction toward the Witch and at the dark figures as she begins to whisper words that I do not understand. Her whispers begin to sound faster and faster as each word echoes over the other. Her whispers start echoing all around me, as if the sound of her voice is carried like a breeze moving directly toward those evil entities. The whispers echo throughout the path by the spirit's energy, somehow stopping them from getting any closer to me. They have been forbidden by a force much greater than what lies inside this darkness. The entities now stand still, held back by the words which cover the dreadful voices heard by those evil dark figures as they wait for instructions given by the Dark Witch. The Witch hovers with a fiery ball of light clutched in her rotted burnt hand, staring directly at us.

Suddenly, the white dress worn by the spirit becomes brighter, and her image starts to change. The image starts to look distorted, bending and twisting while her whispers are still heard all around me. White wings start to appear behind her, and a translucent image starts to form into a shape that I have seen before. Watching through the bright light that once kept me from seeing her shape-shift appear right in front of me, for the first time I can finally watch as the spirit of my Aunt Vera becomes the White Owl. The aura emanates a large motionless light of colors changing within its twisting distorted oval shape. The whispers which echoed through the air had stopped and the White Owl is now standing in front of me. With her wings so beautifully extended out across the path, she stands before me with a light radiating around her just like a dream cascading from a world above. The Dark Entities still stand on each side of me from a distance, somehow held back by the spirit's force which has been so far protecting me from the evil things that stay hidden deep within these dark walls as they feed off my vulnerability and fears.

I stare patiently and wait for the White Owl to make these evil entities go back into the pitch-dark world where they have come from. The Witch still hovers in place with no intention of going back where she came from. The dark figures wait patiently for instructions to continue their quest to drag me into their evil dark realm.

Suddenly, an evil hissing snake-like voice starts to come from the Dark Witch. Immediately I get chills that run throughout my body as I try to understand what is being said. The sound of her voice starts to become clear as every word is followed by a hissing sound throughout the path. "You cannot stop me from taking your soul as I have already taken your brother's," says the Witch.

"You are lying! My brother is still here with me . . . my Aunt Vera has told me so."

Hissing as her voice echoes in every direction from the darkness, "Your Aunt Vera is dead . . . she cannot help you."

"My Aunt Vera is standing here with me . . . She is protecting me from you and those evil dark figures that cannot touch me."

"She is nothing but a bird standing next to you . . . a false profit brought onto you filled with lies," says the Witch.

"*You* are lying . . . You cannot hurt me. My Aunt Vera's spirit who stands next to me is much more powerful than you. Everything that you are saying to me are lies."

The Witch begins to laugh. "She cannot help you to find your way home. You now . . . belong here with us."

As the Witch's laugh is heard echoing from inside the darkness along the path, I look at the White Owl standing with its wings folded back. I am waiting for the White Owl to give me any guidance of what to do next. I know I cannot face what is about to happen from the evil entities who wait patiently to take me into their dark world. A voice begins to follow behind the Witch's laugh. I am unsure what I need to do to get out of this. I know I have to do something now while the White Owl is here protecting me. I just cannot figure out how I am going to get past them. Then I remembered . . . the cross in my front pocket. Aunt Vera gave this to David for protection when he was still with us.

"Oh God . . . I hope it works."

I grab the cross out from inside my front pocket and hold it up to my chin. I put my head down to ask GOD for help. Suddenly . . . the spirit of David is standing right next to me pointing into the darkness. I look in both directions to where the entities are. Something is starting to happen . . . something terrifying is going on with those dark figures. Their heads are shaking from side to side in rapid motion. Their eyes begin to look like black lines moving across their distorted monkey faces. Their heads start to become blurry, almost disappearing from their bodies. So terrifying to watch, I have to look away.

Something happened when I took the cross out of my pocket. David had this fear of the cross. He believed that everything would become worse if he kept it with him. He did not want to provoke what was happening to him at the time. He believed the Dark Entities had scared him into getting rid of it, forcing him to hide the cross in a safe place. Why or how did the cross end up inside the old wooden record player? If the spirit in the White Owl is holding them back from coming any closer to me, why has the cross become a threat to the Entities?

I suddenly see my brother's spirit pointing into the darkness behind me. This could be a way to escape. I have become frightened and anxious, unsure if it is safe for me to walk into the same darkness where the

Entities have come from. Hesitating with so much fear, I turn to look at the evil Dark Witch. I see her rotted burnt hand raising a ball of light high above into the air. Her long thin strands of hair, resembling black smoke, twist and flow, becoming translucent from the light radiating off her hand. I have to go where my brother's spirit pointed me in the direction to where I must go. The White Owl suddenly starts to back away from me, acting strangely. Something is wrong. The White Owl looks at David's spirit and then looks at me.

Feeling anxious, I immediately call out, "We have to go." The White Owl just stands there looking at me.

Frustrated, I ask, "What's wrong? We need to go this way. My brother's spirit is pointing for us to go in this direction."

The Owl moves back and forth as if trying to tell me something. I look at my brother's spirit, knowing I am being led into safety, but something is not right. The spirit turns to where the Witch was and then looks back at me. I sense a strange look between my brother's spirit and the Witch. I back away from my brother's spirit and suddenly see his face become one of those faces of those dark figures—smiling with its rotted teeth. Now I know why the White Owl was trying to warn me about what was happening. This was not really a spirit trying to protect me, but a Dark Entity leading me into the darkness. My stomach starts to hurt from so much fear of the Dark Entities trying to pull me into their world.

I have no choice but to stay with the White Owl, which is used by my Aunt Vera as a vessel channeling between this dark path and where it comes from. Its presence here keeps me safe until my Aunt Vera comes back from where she has gone, using the White Owl to shape-shift back.

Surrounded by so much evil, I begin to feel overwhelmed by the horror that has started to rise from within the darkness as it tries to take control of me just to put an end to my existence. The White Owl begins to move strangely again, making me feel that it senses something terrifying is starting to happen. I look at the Owl closely while keeping my eyes on the Entities and the Witch holding her fiery ball of light. I continue to feel the nervousness inside my stomach, almost needing to vomit again. I have no choice other than to wait for something terrible to happen while watching for any signs of danger.

Wait . . . the White Owl is starting to change. I partly cover my eyes so they won't become irritated from the bright abstract colors radiating from her body. I suddenly see the lady in the white gown standing in front of me. "Aunt Vera . . . you're back," I shouted.

Just as the spirit of my Aunt Vera returned, I saw the spirit whom I thought to be my brother still standing at the edge of the path suddenly put its head down and disappear into the darkness.

"I have come back to take you away from them," said Aunt Vera.

"What is happening? Why do the Witch and the dark figures act strange when I show the cross?"

"The cross was given to me to keep the evil spirits away, a powerful symbol that came from another world where the Angels who are dressed in white protect the innocent souls that have been abandoned by the world you now live in. This cross was used to exorcise the Dark Entities that have attached themselves to a soul, whether living or trapped between both worlds."

"Like my brother before he died," I replied.

"Yes, Robert . . . Like your brother."

"But . . . David did not use it to protect himself. He was scared to keep it with him."

As I look down, I am feeling sad, thinking that he would have been safe if he had held on to it.

"Robert . . . he was scared because of being constantly haunted by nightmares and the curse that was placed upon him by Barbara."

I take a deep breath, feeling sad about David not realizing that he could have been protected by the cross.

Sudden changes within the pathway start to occur, and strange voices begin to echo from all around me. Aunt Vera's spirit tells me to grab her hand. The Entities, along with the Witch's chant, become louder and louder as the mist starts to move through the path, as if there is more unprecedented evil ready to make itself known. The evil dark figures start to circle while continuing to rapidly move their heads from side to side. The Witch continues to hold her fiery ball into the air as her hair-like strands of black smoke hover above—like snakes swaying back and forth from inside the darkness. The thick mist swirls around the Witch's black gown with a dark shadow moving along the ground as it gets closer to us.

Across the path from the Witch, a large pitch-black figure starts to form from within the darkness. Everything around me has become chaotic as the energy has become cold and dark. The spirit of my Aunt Vera is watching the large pitch-black figure move into the light near the Witch. The Witch is guiding this dark figure with its light coming from the fiery ball. I am terrified even though my aunt's spirit is with me. Something evil is being drawn out from the same world these evil entities have come from. Something much more evil than what is inside this path standing before me has been brought here to help drag me into its realm. At this moment, I can see a little boy's spirit standing off to the side of me. He is watching and waiting, just as I am for this pitch-dark figure to show itself. I look at my Aunt Vera and she nods her head to let me know that the little boy's spirit is actually David and not the evil entity that pretended to be him. Everything is still chaotic all around me as this pitch-dark energy starts to form on this poorly lit path. I look toward the Dark Witch wanting to stop her from bringing whatever it was into the pathway. Instead, I see two rings appear, circling around her in opposite directions just like before when I first saw this evil image standing from a distance, unaware of what it was going to do to me. The rings are helping this pitch-dark figure to appear by feeding its evil energy into it, making it stronger.

Aunt Vera clutches my hand knowing I want to yell at the Witch to stop. I can still see the image of my brother's spirit watching. However, I now see another spirit of a little boy whom I had recognized earlier standing next to Dr. Scott inside this nightmare. They both seem to be waiting for something, as if they, like me, are waiting to be free from this nightmare. The cold air moves around as the dark figure is brought forth by the Witch while the thick mist swirls above, bringing a stench in the air that is becoming stronger as this black mass starts to take form. *"Oh, my God . . . I can see who the pitch-dark figure is."*

A lady finally appears from the darkness, also standing with a black gown draped along the ground and black hair covering part of her face. Aunt Vera looks at me and says, "It is Barbara."

"What . . . Barbara, but . . . but, how?" I am totally puzzled as I look at my aunt.

Aunt Vera replies, "It is the forthcoming of the *Dark Evil One* who controls her evil entities."

CHAPTER 15

THE DARK EVIL ONE

REMEMBERING HOW BARBARA caused so much pain in our family, never taking any responsibility for the tragedy she had caused for me and my parents.

Her intent to inflict pain on our family seems to have been caused by something that happened long before my brother and I were ever born. With no apparent reason behind her evil intention, I have only seen the pain she caused—seeking out those who are unable to protect themselves from someone who is so dark and evil. Having to face this alone, I have fallen into her daunting nightmares and surreal images that have led to this endless dark path by Barbara, only to use all that she has created to take control of me and whoever else she wants to drag into her world. She seems connected to this dark world using her witchcraft through those dark figures hiding within these dark walls to watch me. With having no way of leaving this dreadful place, she has kept those Entities fed by my fear and anxiety, which buildup while I stand here scared of what is about to happen.

My parents never spoke about Aunt Barbara until my father went to her home wanting to know why Uncle Eddie "did what he did," causing my brother's death. Barbara kept herself secluded from the outside world. It was only after my parents talked about her involvement in the practice of Black Magic, which she used against those by whom she felt threatened, did all of that come to light—so to speak. That day, my father left her house without any answers to what he went looking for. Unfortunately, he brought back home something evil, which still haunts us even after my Aunt Vera attempted to rid this Entity of its attachment to our home. Two years later, Barbara continues to be responsible for everything that I have been going through so far.

Today, nothing makes any sense of why Barbara wants to take me away from my parents. I am confused about so many things happening at this moment. I have so many questions that were unanswered, yet I am holding a cross that is a threat to those Dark Entities. Feeling frustrated and scared, I just keep thinking, *I don't even know how the cross and the drawing ended up with me. I don't even know why I ended up in a place with no way of getting back.*

Barbara's dark spirit stands at a distance with the Entities she has created by her side. Aunt Vera's spirit is the only thing holding back what could be devastating and horrifying to come. As I'm standing here feeling trapped, my fear suddenly starts to turn into anger. I must force myself not to give into fear and refuse to allow all the evil that surrounds me to feed off my frustration. Somehow, this only makes me more vulnerable to the Dark Entities watching me at this moment.

Still, I cannot stop myself from placing the blame on those who have stopped me from going back to the life into which I was born. Then, something strange begins to happen to me. Feeling sad, scared and with an uncontrollable feeling of wanting to cry, it's as if my emotions are being controlled by something here. A sudden thought of resentment starts to come over me, turning my fear that has been kept inside for so long into the anger I tried so hard to push away. Remembered thoughts start to go through my head. An overwhelming feeling of negative thoughts and blame begin to emerge through memories when my brother was alive. Feeling frustrated, I would never have thought my childhood would have to revolve around the travesty of all the dark images and strange nightmares intentionally brought on by the same person who has come back to cause more pain to my family. I have never done anything wrong that deserves the torment orchestrated [1] by such an evil person. Yet here she stands before me still wanting to do harm.

I feel this uncontrollable anger along with a voice coming from inside my head. This dark spirit whom my Aunt Vera calls the "Dark One" seems to be controlling my emotions. The voice inside my head is not the slithering voice coming from the Dark Witch, but a voice so terrifying I begin to get cold chills going through my body. I look at the spirit of Aunt Vera and ask her, "What does the *Dark Evil One* wants from us?"

"Listen . . . Do you hear?" said Aunt Vera.

"I do . . . I hear her inside my head. She sounds like a whistling screech moving throughout the night's air."

"Yes, a ghostly sound of lost souls moving through the trees blowing into the darkness."

Aunt Vera continues to watch Barbara (*The Evil One*) from a distance.

Barbara, like the *Witch* who was created from her own image, stands like a dark spirit with her black gown draped along the ground. Black hair flowing over her shoulders and large dark eyes looking toward us as the Witch hovers next to her like a shadow. Barbara and the Witch are the same Entities driven by fear, although Barbara uses the Witch's eyes to see into her dark world, watching over those souls that have become lost inside the darkness or displaced by an unforeseen tragedy.

Barbara, who appears out of the darkness, is now whispering in a wicked, high-pitch voice like a strong breeze whistling through the darkness. I turn to my Aunt Vera's spirit and stare at her, feeling terrified about what is being said by the voice coming from inside my head. The voice that I believe to be coming from the *Dark Evil One* is trying to tell me something. The chilling whispers are unclear. I continue to look at my aunt's spirit and know I am not the only one who can hear the wicked voice.

The voice finally leaves my head, the high-pitch sound of the whispers stops, and my hearing starts to return. I start to realize that I have heard the humming before after losing my hearing when I first ended up alone inside this pathway, smelling the stench of old rotted mold throughout this darkness. Now I believe that my first experience of being led here was by the presence of Barbara's evil intent of trying to communicate with me. Fortunately, she became unsuccessful without having enough control over her evil entities to help.

Is this why she is here now? She needed the evil Dark Witch along with the dark figures to finally help her evil spirit make its way into this dark path? The connection between the Dark Witch and Barbara had to be strong enough to allow Barbara's presence to move through the gateway that separates this dark world from the outside world where she controls all the evil that lurks behind the pitch-dark walls around me.

A terrifying voice begins to be heard throughout the path. Still, unable to understand what is being said, the whistling sounds of her words finally become clear as her evil presence starts to adjust to this world that I am desperately trying to escape. While Barbara is slowly being drawn in by the energy of the evil entities she has created, the others are still held back by the presence of my Aunt Vera's spirit holding my hand while my other hand holds tightly onto the cross.

The *Dark Evil One* whispers in its wicked voice, "I finally meet you, Robert . . . I wanted to talk to you . . . I won't hurt you."

She is laughing with a large mouth resembling those of her dark figures.

"No, you hurt my family . . . I wish you would go away forever."

The *Dark Evil One* says, "Robert . . . I am here to help you . . . do you want to live free from all the nightmares that this lady who stands beside you has caused you and your family?"

Her loud, wicked whispers are heard throughout the pathway.

"You are a liar . . . You are here to take me away from my family."

Aunt Vera interrupts, "Leave. Go back to where you have come from."

The *Dark One* replies, "Quiet, Witch . . . this lady is not your Aunt Vera, Robert . . . she is a witch that cannot be trusted . . . come with me."

"Never . . . just leave. I will never go with you."

I hold onto the cross above my head hoping that all this will stop. The *Dark Witch* standing next to Barbara holds the fiery ball above her hair-like strands of black smoke, hovering above, somehow keeping Barbara's dark spirit close by. I quickly turn around as I felt a sudden tug on my shirt behind me. I noticed this little boy standing in front of me. I knew right away it had to be my brother's spirit. I can smell the scent of lavender once again filling the air while covering the stench of those evil dark figures as they try to make their way closer to me.

David's spirit looks at me, pointing to my front pocket. I know the only thing left inside my pocket is the drawing. I pull the drawing out of my front pocket, placing the cross between my lips to find out what he wanted me to look at.

"*OH MY GOD*, It's . . . it's . . . " I turn my head, looking at my Aunt Vera, feeling so confused about what is in the drawing. I ask my brother's spirit, "Why did you want me to see this?" He slowly put his head down without saying anything. I could not believe what I was looking at.

I felt betrayed . . . a warning by my brother's spirit. A feeling of disappointment at what I saw inside the drawing. How could this be . . . ?

How can he be part of everything that has been happening to me, so far? I just do not see how or why he would be part of Evil inside this pathway wanting to do harm toward me and my family. Even though I was unable to tell him everything when I first saw him sitting inside his office, I would never have expected him to be a part of what I have been experiencing. If all this is true, he must have already known what I have been going through.

The spirit of my brother suddenly disappears leaving behind more questions about this terrible nightmare. My Aunt Vera's spirit is unable to tell me everything, as if I had to figure out all of this on my own. Aunt Vera stands here protecting me, yet she cannot help me find my way back home where I belong. I must trust her, unknowing what the outcome will be after facing the evil that waits patiently inside this pathway.

Still confused and upset of what I saw inside the drawing, I could not stop thinking about whose face was on the paper. The face is a little faint, yet I know who it was. This warning shown to me by my brother's spirit had made it difficult for me to think that I was looking at Dr. Scott's face partially sketched behind the Witch in the drawing. How is he connected to Barbara? I then remember seeing a framed picture of a little girl, a little boy, and a man standing behind them, hanging up on his wall inside his office. I never got a chance to ask Dr. Scott about the picture. I asked Aunt Vera's spirit about Dr. Scott, even though I knew she was unable to tell me about certain things that would unexpectedly appear. All I can do at this moment is watch everything around me and try to find a way of getting out of here.

Surrounded by the Dark figures on one side of me and Barbara along with the Witch on the other side, I can only hope Aunt Vera's spirit will find us a way to escape. I placed the drawing back into my pocket and placed the cross close to my chest. The smell of lavender has disappeared, and the stench of rotted mold still lingers throughout the darkness. The cold mist continues to flow along the dark path letting me know of the evil presence that still resides here.

Barbara's dark spirit starts to move closer toward us. Unaware of her intentions, I quickly look at my aunt's spirit unsure of what to do next. The *Dark Witch* follows beside Barbara as the cold mist swirls, making these two large rings of mist rotating in opposite direction moving around them. The *Witch* clutches onto the fiery ball creating a light making her rotted face visible as the translucent strands black smoke emanate from her pitch-black dress. My aunt's spirit assures me that I will be safe standing with her. I feel as if I am waiting for something terrifying to appear. The spirit stands here with me as she continues to keep Entities away from me. I force myself to stay calm and wait even though I am so frightened; not knowing what I will be facing if I cannot escape from the evil that waits so patiently.

The spirit of my Aunt Vera points and tells me to see into the darkness across the path from where we stand. I start to see an image appear. The same image I saw before when a little boy's spirit, whom I mistakenly thought to be my brother, pointed to an image showing a woman pleading to the man as his voice became louder and louder. I was saddened by this image, not knowing why this little boy had led me farther onto the path just to show me two people I had never seen before. I never knew who the little boy was or why he forces me to watch the image of this strange, mean man. I only thought of the little boy as being a lost soul from a different time and place trying to show me something he remembered from the life he once lived.

Now, however, my aunt's spirit shows me the same image. I am still unsure of who those people are. I ask her, "Why do you show me these people?"

"This is why you are here," answered her spirit. "You told me I'm here because I was unable to return to my body when I became disembodied while sleeping, allowing myself to be dragged into this dark path."

"That is true, Robert. However, this is why Barbara has led you here."

"Why . . . ?" I am so confused.

"I am unable to tell you. I can only show you."

Aunt Vera's spirit continues to have me watch the image as it appears in front of me. I do not understand why I must see these people inside the image when Barbara stands patiently ready to unleash the evil that she has created to possess me. This has nothing to do with what is about to happen. My anxiety returns, becoming overwhelming, along with the thought of wasting our time watching other people, when we need to get away from something much more terrifying. Voices coming from the *Dark Entities* move throughout the path as the overlapping sounds of the ungodly whispers try to draw my attention away from the image being shown to me by my aunt's spirit. The dark spirits are trying to keep me from looking at the image. Suddenly, the image of the people becomes more vivid, and their voices are starting to be heard.

CHAPTER 16
UNKNOWN IMAGES

NOTHING COULD PREPARE ME for what I am about to find out as I soon face some truth behind my entrapment here inside such a dark place, along with images that send chills throughout my body.

The sound of the man's voice becomes loud. With his deep and demanding voice, he stands directly in front of the lady yelling at her. He looks very tall with his fedora hat and clothing that looks like what my grandfather used to wear. When I first saw the image of the two, I knew they were from a different time and place. I was saddened by what I saw the first time when the lady in the yellow dress seemed to be pleading to the man. Having to watch the image, I did not understand who or what I was looking at for the first time. I suddenly recognized the man inside the image.

"Wait . . . I know who that is."

I saw that same man with the little boy and the little girl inside the picture hanging up on the wall behind Dr. Scott's chair when I was inside his office. I found it strange to see this person who is close to Dr. Scott appear to me as a bad person. However, the picture I stared at on the wall could be just an image that stuck inside my head, making me think that this person could be part of my nightmare—a nightmare I cannot seem to wake up from.

Is it possible that I am imagining everything along with the drawing that sits inside my pocket? This whole time, trapped inside this dreadful place filled with so many horrible things following me around as I wander aimlessly inside the dark, could be all inside my head. I still cannot seem to figure out if this is all real or I am just having a long, drawn-out nightmare.

Having the drawing in my possession, I do see more things recorded on this paper by my brother than what I saw when David's life was slowly being taken away by all the bad things which now stand before me. The sketches are more of a warning now to help me get through this horrible nightmare, although the images have not made my presence here any better. I notice the images that appear in front of me or inside the drawing become "some sort" of a sign, showing me those who have been used by the darkness to draw me further away from the life I have only known.

At this moment, my thoughts about Dr. Scott have changed and everything he said to me were only lies. Looking at the drawing now, the partially sketched picture of Dr. Scott behind the Witch in David's drawing, was a warning. The man inside the image yelling at the lady must be a part of Dr. Scott's family. Somehow, the connection between Dr. Scott and the Dark Witch becomes involved. I do not see how there could be a connection.

Suddenly, I can hear the man inside the image tell the lady that you cannot leave. The lady pleads to the man to let her go. She begs the man, "Please leave, my son will be coming home . . . Please . . . Please."

"No, I cannot leave," says the man, with such an evil look on his face. "Please, just leave us alone."

"You have been chosen by him . . . I am here to make sure this gets done," says the man.

"*NO . . . Oh, GOD . . . NO . . .* Please leave us alone." The lady is pleading to the man to leave.

I put my head down trying to figure out why the man I see in the picture is talking to the lady like this. *Why? Why? . . . I don't understand. What is the man going to do to the lady?*

"Please, Aunt Vera, why do you show me this and not tell me who or what that man is doing there at that house? What does all this have to do with why I am here?"

I suddenly see the man inside the image grab a hammer. Suddenly the lady falls to the floor pleading to the man to stop. He then lifts the hammer over his head striking her violently on the side of her face where he proceeds to strike her several more times while she lays bleeding on her kitchen floor. I then see the little boy come walking into the house where he finds the man dragging his mother across the floor.

Oh No . . . This is the same little boy that appears standing next to Dr. Scott along this path. The little boy was the one who first showed me the image of this lady and man. *Oh, my God . . . What is he going to do to the little boy?*

The boy walks in and the man lets go of the lady and grabs the little boy. He quickly grabs the little boy by the arm and strikes him on the side of his head. The man then drags the mother and the little boy out into the backyard which seems to be late at night.

This is shocking . . . Having to watch the man whom I saw in the picture inside Dr. Scott's office with the two small children doing something so evil to these people, it's no wonder that this little boy's spirit whom I have been seeing here inside this dark path must have become lost after his death, just like my brother David. Something or someone must have brought the little boy here.

This horrific image shown to me by the spirit of my aunt leads me to believe that this could be a sign of what I am supposed to be looking for. At least, that is why I am here. The spirit of the little boy and the spirit of my brother are connected somehow through this nightmare, which Barbara has created. A nightmare manifesting in a world where she hides the souls of those who have suffered, becoming the ones that stand by her side now. Barbara has brought herself here inside this dark path to have me become one of those dark figures. Fortunately, she has not possessed my soul yet. By her taking control of me, she will also have the souls of my brother and the little boy who appeared to me unexpectedly.

If the spirit of my aunt keeps me safe, there is no way Barbara can drag me into her world. Still, the thought of being completely safe is not certain until she has vanished into the darkness, unable to hurt anyone else again. Unknowing what I will have to face, I must find out who the man I just saw murdering the lady and the little boy. This could help me find out why the little boy has come to me and why Dr. Scott was sketched next to the evil Dark Witch inside the drawing.

The image of the gruesome crime finally disappears, leaving behind a feeling of disbelief and sadness toward the family that was murdered. I still cannot understand why these people are part of what is going on with me.

The spirit of Aunt Vera continues to stand near me as my body shakes from being so cold, along with an overwhelming fear of still having to face Barbara. Again, I ask Aunt Vera who were those people inside the images that were shown to me? She looks at me for a moment, as if she were looking right through me. I thought about the man inside the picture frame hanging up in Dr. Scott's office. Then I thought about the sketch of Dr. Scott's face in the drawing. I cannot figure out how Dr. Scott's face would be partially sketched behind the Witch in the picture. Suddenly, I go right back to thinking about the man in the picture and how he is related to Dr. Scott. Nothing seems to make sense. I have no way of finding out when Dr. Scott only appears to me as an image inside this dark path. When Dr. Scott does appear to me, the little boy is standing next to him. Would Dr. Scott have to be already dead if he is here with the little boy? I look at my aunt's spirit, begging her to give me answers. Still nothing. I continue to look at her, thinking how everyone here who has appeared to me so far is not living anymore. I put my head down feeling so incredibly sad. I then ask Aunt Vera, "How did you die?"

I need to know how Aunt Vera suddenly died when I never had known her to even be sick—ever. She lifted her hand and pointed to where Barbara and the Witch are watching patiently and waiting. She says, "Them."

I looked at her and said, "My mother told me you died from pneumonia in the hospital."

"That is true . . . look into the darkness," said Aunt Vera's spirit.

She points off into the darkness once again and shows me another image of herself sleeping in bed at home with a shadow-like figure standing over her. Inside this image shows her breathing in a strange thick mist hovering all around her. I look back toward the Witch standing next to Barbara and see the same thick mist expelling from where they are. The shadow-like figure I saw inside the image must have been the Dark Witch that was standing over my Aunt Vera that night as she breathed in the thick mist that caused her pneumonia and death. I turn to the spirit of Aunt Vera and said, "Barbara killed you . . .

"Why would she want to kill you? Is this why you are here with me? To stop Barbara?"

I feel as if everything is becoming more confusing. Even though nothing seems to make sense, it is clear why the spirits have appeared to me—because they have all been a part of my life. This nightmare has drawn in everyone who has been connected to me one way or another. Barbara has somehow impacted those souls passing through this nightmare, knowing that they have come to help me. Even those who have passed on from this life have appeared to me only wanting to become free from Barbara's dark world. Misguided by her evil intentions, she has led the souls of those whom I have cared for through this pathway, which connects me to her dark realm. Barbara seeks out my soul along with all the significance of living a normal life only to keep me here forever.

I honestly believe my chances of returning to a normal life I desperately want is assured now that I am finding what I was brought here to do through the images that have already appeared to me. The signs are there for me to put everything in the perspective of leaving behind this dreadful place, along with all the bad things that stay hidden inside its darkness. All that remains within this dark path must stay here, never returning to cause any more of the suffering that it has already inflicted on my family. This includes Barbara and all that she created by taking away the curse placed upon me and my brother, and never mentioning her name again. The truth of why I am here has not completely become clear, however the images appearing to me will help make everything clearer as time starts to move within this dark path. These *evil entities* have frozen time within these walls made of pitch-black darkness that run along this path. There seems to be no movement as far as time here inside this horrible place. Life here does not seem to exist. Everything here is devoured by the negative energy that leaves behind an unsettling infinite darkness. *Life outside this dark, dreadful cold place can never be taken away from me. I will not give up what belongs to me, which is happiness and the family that loves me.*

Shaking from the fear that still goes through my body, I hold on to the cross under my chin and wait for any sign coming from my aunt's spirit. Everything has come to a standstill as the Entities watch on from a distance. I have not seen any movement coming from either side of me; only the coldness and the stench of rotted mold lingering in the air. The last image of the people appearing to me has disappeared, giving me a sense of how parts of this nightmare are coming together. Still, an overwhelming feeling of anxiety has come over me waiting for something unexpected to happen. I can feel a pain come from my stomach just as it always does when something bad is about to happen. All I can do is wait.

I have not felt the presence of my brother's spirit here with me since he warned me about Dr. Scott. There had been moments I thought he was here with me, and other times he was an illusion made up by the *evil entities* coming from this place. I suddenly thought about how I would hear the whispers coming from David after his death. I remembered hearing David's whispers inside my head when I would wake up from sleepwalking during the middle of the night. I could hear David whispering these words that have always stayed with me like memories. Unfortunately, I was unaware during that time that he was trying to warn me from a place that I would now be facing with him. The whispers I heard from David are the only thing that I would have left between us. I can still hear him say, *"I was living with the fear that was coming from within myself when, in fact, the experiences I was going through were all memories of what happened to me. So scared of what I saw, of what I thought to be just a part of what I was going through only to find out that I was an illusion of my own existence . . . "*

I believe David's *"Fear within himself"* manifested from the nightmares created the Entities he had sketched on a piece of paper. What *"I was going through were all memories of what happened to me,"* were caused by the curse placed upon him, which led up to his death. And *"Finding out that I was an illusion of my own existence"* would become a place where he found himself lost inside this dark path, unaware of his own death.

Barbara knew she led him here trapped inside this dark world. Fortunately, she was unable to completely possess him. Barbara did not have complete control of David. However, she left him lost between both worlds, unaware of him still having a connection with me. Those whispers I heard during the dark hours of the night were not only a sign of a warning, but a sign of a soul that needed peace.

I know . . . what I need to do now: I must free myself along with my brother's spirit from this dreadful place. I must continue to find my way home and help my brother and this little boy become free.

CHAPTER 17

REUNION

DARK ENERGY SEEMS TO BE getting stronger within this path while the Entities begin to move in closer, causing me to think that something evil is starting to evolve as the truth becomes a little clearer.

A screeching voice is heard echoing from Barbara as the Dark Witch hovers by her side holding the fiery ball, which continues to form these two large transparent rings circling in opposite directions. The rings look like large halos close behind the Witch as she is devising a dark energy that is growing stronger as it devours those lost souls coming from deep within the darkness surrounding this path. As Barbara and the Witch move gradually toward us, they still seem to hesitate to get any closer. They seem to fear something, but I am unsure what it could be.

Something is starting to appear next to Barbara, another dark figure. The image is blurry, but the energy coming from Barbara has summoned something else into her world. I move in closer to the spirit of my aunt who is standing in front of me and I whisper, "Who could that be?" I am so exhausted at the thought of having to face something else—another unknown entity.

As the image becomes clearer, I soon know whose image it is. This familiar image has become a part of a world driven by fear. A fear created by Barbara as she continues to feed off any kind of life brought in from the outside world. An image becoming more of a warning than that of a memory. I have yet to understand why I am surrounded by images that seem to be a part of this dark world connected to Barbara. Having to face such an evil person leads me to believe that she will use anyone or anything to bring me closer to her empty darkness. Nevertheless, I can see the same person that was supposed to understand what I am going through. The same person that I was supposed to trust and would help me. Now, this person stands before me as one of Barbara's followers to help draw me further into her realm.

Watching alongside the dark spirits, I now see Dr. Scott's image manifest from the dark figure standing next to Barbara. Dr. Scott's image is still vague as it tends to appear in and out, making it difficult to clearly see him. Yet, I know enough that I am looking at Dr. Scott, who is somehow connected to Barbara. I have seen him appear on this path before along with the little boy. Dr. Scott always seems to appear and disappear for a moment by moment.

I was confused to see him appear here until I saw the drawing of his face sketched next to the Witch. I am now understanding that anything coming from the drawing is for the purpose of communication between me and my brother—to warn me of those who have been a part of Barbara's evil intent. This is why Dr. Scott could be connected to what is happening to me. I can do nothing but wait. The whispers are still echoing and screeching like a wicked breeze moving through the path, causing the image of Dr. Scott to appear a little clearer. I continue to stay close to my aunt's spirit, asking her what is about to happen. She turns to me and quietly says, "Barbara is strengthening the negative energy within this place."

I can feel myself becoming overwhelmed by everything that is going on around me. The unexpected fears and anxiety of all the bad things about to happen at this moment begin to come together, intentionally creating a disruption to lure me away from my aunt's spirit. Aunt Vera starts to push me behind her long white gown to make sure I am not harmed in any way. Voices echoing all around. The Entities gradually moving toward us. The images of Dr. Scott still standing with Barbara, only now he is appearing with each hand on the shoulders of my brother David and the little boy as he keeps them standing in front of him, side by side, close together.

They both stand in front of Dr. Scott's image, as if he is keeping them from going anywhere. The little boy is just like my brother, trapped inside this dark path, unable to become free from this dark world. I want to do something to make Dr. Scott let them go. I beg my aunt's spirit to help set them free, and she just looks at me. Again, I beg the spirit to make Dr. Scott release them. Dr. Scott does not respond as his image appears to still be blurry. It seems to appear in and out as if it has not completely made it into this world yet. He holds onto the boys' spirits, becoming a distraction, while Barbara and the Witch continue to cause chaos throughout the path. The Dark Figures, with their evil monkey faces partially covered, move back and forth from a distance. The chanting whispers are heard echoing from the Entities as they wait and watch from each side of the path.

I stand behind Aunt Vera's spirit, still firmly holding onto the cross. I feel helpless just standing here. There is nothing I can do to help my brother. How can they be held against their will if they are already trapped inside this path? I am about to put my head down and think about how much I want to go home. No sooner than I start to put my head down than my aunt's spirit tells me to look toward Barbara. I see Barbara and Dr. Scott standing next to each other as the spirits of David and the murdered little boy seem to be standing helpless, unable to leave. Now, all of a sudden, I am getting a vision of the little boy and little girl inside the picture hanging on the wall in Dr. Scott's office. I look again toward Barbara and Dr. Scott, realizing that those two kids in the picture with the man are Dr. Scott and Barbara. Chills run through my body as I stand there looking at them. Could Barbara and Dr. Scott be siblings, and the man in the picture be their father? How could this be possible?

Dr. Scott spoke about a little boy he saw in his parents' backyard. He also spoke about him and his parents moving into the same home where a mother and child were found dead in their backyard. I also remember Dr. Scott saying that the father was found guilty of the crime years later. Could this be the mother and child I saw inside the image shown to me by the spirit of the little boy and then by my Aunt Vera? I am confused as I stand looking into the darkness along the path. How could Dr. Scott's father be the same man inside the image hitting the lady and the little boy on the head with the hammer if the father of the little boy was found guilty of the crime? I would never have guessed that the small kids inside the picture were Barbara and Dr. Scott.

I do not understand why my brother and I are part of their nightmare. Why are Dr. Scott and Barbara trying to drag us away into their world? What would cause those people to hate us so much and take us away from the life we have just started?

Barbara seems to feed off our souls using Dr. Scott as she did with my Uncle Eddie. I don't understand why Uncle Eddie came over to our house that night causing my brother's death. I don't think he really knew why he came over that night. Everyone around her seems to become consumed by Barbara's hate, lost in her dark world, not aware of what she is doing to innocent people around her. I believe her practice of Black Magic has completely submerged her deep into darkness, and she is unable to return from a world she has created—a dark world used as a pathway to capture the *souls* around her.

Barbara must be stopped, and I need to free David's spirit. I believe I can also help the little boy escape as well. I ask my aunt's spirit if there is a way to stop what is happening.

The spirit replies, "There *is* a way to stop them. Break the circle that strengthens the evil that Barbara has brought into this path."

"How can I break the circle? They are too powerful, and I cannot leave your side."

"Only *you* can stop them," says the spirit.

"I don't know how . . . I just think they are too terrifying to face."

Now I feel myself wanting to give up. I am unable to bring myself to face this evil that has been daunting me. The only thing standing between me and those Entities is my aunt's spirit. I feel as if Barbara is trying to lure me closer to her by using the spirits of David and the little boy.

I am desperately trying to ignore those whispering voices heard throughout this dark path, making it difficult for me to keep out of my head. The spirit candles running along each side of me flicker as the stench of those Entities continues to fill the air. It is difficult for me to breathe in through my nose and mouth. I can only hope to smell the lavender once again in the air when my brother's presence returns.

Chaos from the dark energy continues to be a disruption. The echoes, the whispers, and the evil presence all around me move in and out from within those dark walls that keep me trapped here. Barbara hovers next to her brother as the Witch continues to hold up its fiery ball, creating a dark energy that surrounds me and my aunt's spirit. I can only wait for a chance to help stop what is happening. Instead, I am forced to stand by and watch all the evil. It is hesitant to come any closer.

I ask my aunt's spirit why the Entities seem to be afraid. Then, it occurs to me—maybe it's the cross I am holding. The cross was sent to me by David. He had placed it in a wooden record player box wrapped up in an old dusty cloth. I slowly take the cloth out of my pocket while holding the cross against my chest with my other hand. I look at the cloth and realize it matches the white gown of my aunt's spirit. I am beginning to understand why I am here and why I have experienced so many things inside this path. This is my destiny.

My destiny is to be the voice of those who have been a part of my life. I was led into this darkness by the disembodied voices wanting my help. Instead, I was interfered with by Barbara's intention to keep my spirit from returning to my physical body as I heard voices were calling out to me.

Unfortunately, Barbara failed. Instead, she has kept me from returning to the only life I knew as she tries to take my soul back with her to her empty dark realm. She just caused my soul to be pushed further into the darkness, becoming lost. As I became disembodied from one of my nightmares, just before ending up here inside this dreadful place, Barbara has somehow closed the opening used to bridge my world and this other strange, mysterious world of darkness, drawing my spirit along this dark path. Even Barbara has found that the darkness is too powerful and cannot be manipulated by someone who still exists outside this world. The dark path has become a place to hold the lost souls just before Barbara tries to lead them into her realm. Barbara has failed to finish her task—the ultimate reason why she has come here.

Aunt Vera's spirit so far has kept me and my brother's spirit, along with that of the murdered little boy, from being dragged into Barbara's horrible world, making it difficult for her to complete this transition. Barbara has failed to understand I have the most important piece to this nightmare. Although I am just a little boy, the spirits of those who have cared for me still live through all my memories. Unlike Barbara, who affects everything with the rotten stench she leaves behind as she holds onto those who eventually become part of the darkness. Watching Barbara and Dr. Scott reunite to take away the most important person from my life has become overwhelming. I can feel every memory drain from me as I see David's spirit become vulnerable. I fear, if I do nothing, I will lose my brother forever, along with the little boy who stands next to him.

I put the cloth next to the spirit of my aunt. She smiles and says, "I'll always be with you."

I start to panic. "I don't understand. Are you leaving me here all alone?"

She looks at me with a light shining from her eyes. "You have already found what you have come for."

"I still don't understand what you are telling me."

Aunt Vera's spirit whispers, "You have the most important piece to stop this nightmare."

I become dazed from all the thoughts going through my head. Withdrawing myself from everything around me, I slowly reach into my pocket and take out the drawing. I hold it in my hand, feeling sad, but I somehow know what I need to do. I stare into the dark path, slowly turning to look at Dr. Scott's spirit.

"There is one thing I do remember from what you told me when I went to see you in your office: *Never hold stuff inside too long because you will eventually surround yourself with really bad things that will keep you from being happy.*"

I kneel down to the ground and place the drawing over the burning spirit candle. I watch the paper catch fire while the ash disappears into the air. I am incredibly sad to know that this drawing belonged to David, the only thing that he loved to do when he was alive. I can hear all the noises around me once again. But something is different. The whispering voices have stopped. I look over to where Barbara is, and Dr. Scott is no longer there. The Dark Witch is still next to Barbara and the Dark Figures on the other side of me have stopped moving erratically back and forth. The evil chants echoing throughout the path are gone. Everything around me is very still. I do not see my brother's spirit or the little boy anywhere near me.

I realize I am still holding onto the cross. I feel as though I need to do one more thing; I just have not figured out what I still need to do. I stare at the cross in my hand, trying to decide what I must do to stop all the evil things from keeping me from returning home.

Suddenly I can smell the lavender. Oh how nice it is to smell something else other than the stench that lingers in the air from those Entities. I smile and look at my aunt's spirit, knowing David is nearby. I rub the cross with my fingers, moving it around in the palm of my hand. I am still unsure if I am going to escape from the Entities who still watch me from a distance. I continue to look at the cross, getting ready to put it back in my pocket. I look across the path and David's spirit appears, standing halfway out of the darkness. I look at Aunt Vera's spirit next to me and I nod my head to see if it is okay for me to approach David as he stands waiting just behind the spirit candles. David is looking down at the ground just outside of the darkness along this path. I start to cry uncontrollably as I walk up to him. David's spirit looks up at me with a tear coming down the side of his face. His face looks so bright, as the tear from David sparkles down his cheek. I try to wipe the tears from my eyes, but I cannot seem to keep myself from crying so much. I feel as if all the pain that was kept inside is now pouring uncontrollably out through my tears.

A heaviness inside my chest feels as if the pain is being pulled from me. I can see an aura of translucent light leaving my body while the hurt I felt inside disappears, lifting the heaviness that I have carried for a while. Yet, a numbness remains as this emptiness starts to replace the weight being drained from my spirit. My tears start to diminish and the energy coming from the aura of light leaving my body starts to flow into David's spirit, making his image become more real. I put my hand on David's shoulder and look into his eyes. I wipe the tears off my face as I clear my throat to tell him how I feel.

"David . . . Mom and Dad love you and miss you so much, I wish you could come back."

David looks at me with so much sadness. I take David's hand and place the cross into his palm. I try to keep myself from crying again as I tell him that the cross belonged to him so he can now finally go home. I feel so hurt telling him to go home, knowing his real home was with me and our parents. For a moment, I have forgotten about the Entities that remain inside this pathway with me. While my hand is still on David's shoulder, I turn to look back at the spirit of my Aunt Vera, feeling a sense of peace. As I looked at Aunt Vera's spirit, my hand fell from David's shoulder. I quickly turned, and David was gone. I began to cry once more staring into the darkness where David was standing.

CHAPTER 18
THE RETURNED

HAVING FOUND PEACE inside this nightmare, I still remain lost inside the darkness, unaware of what I will face as I find myself alone waiting with the spirit of my Aunt Vera.

Returning to where Aunt Vera's spirit waits, I ask what has happened to the spirit of the murdered little boy? My aunt's spirit turns to face me and slowly takes my hands.

"Do you remember when I said I will always be with you?"

"Yes . . ."

"I must leave now. Remember, Robert . . . you still need to finish what you came here for." The spirit raises my chin to look at her.

"But . . . but . . . I've already returned the cross and destroyed the drawing, Aunt Vera."

Her spirit speaks in a soft voice, "All your questions will be answered soon, Robert, but you must confront what connects you to your nightmare. You are connected through a channel which allows evil and good, the darkness and the light to come together, creating this world difficult to understand. A spiritual world made up of innocent and ungodly souls unable to coexist with your world. A place where you cannot distinguish what is real and what is not. You can only hope that something so evil is not standing inside the darkness waiting to pull you into a world from which you will never return. This channel must be broken. Your world, and the world Barbara has created, must never cross. Barbara has failed to complete what she had started. Your soul belongs to you. This is why you must stop what is happening now."

I am standing inside this poorly lit path watching everything around me become unhinged as the negative energy hinders my every thought inside my head. The negative energy still lingers while every Dark Entity begins to move closer. Each spirit candle burns out, drawing in the empty, cold darkness, and following close behind, Barbara and the Dark Witch.

The thought of never leaving this place becomes more of a reality than a bad dream. I look down at my empty hands, fearing the worst without having the cross and the drawing to keep me safe. Soon, the spirit of my Aunt Vera will be gone, and the Entities will have what they came here for. I guess fear can really turn into anger, especially when you find yourself with nowhere to run. As I become more vulnerable, I stand with my head down ready to give up. Yet, I still find myself scared with so many questions when the time comes to force myself to leave with the Dark Entities. Deep down inside my heart, I still feel the reinsurance that someone or something is not going to let me fade into darkness forever. If I cannot stop the darkness from taking my soul, will I leave with the memories that I have come into this horrible place with? Will I still be haunted by the nightmares when I close my eyes forever? Will "Hope" exist, and I can look forward to the next life? Or will the evil which stands before me take every bit of my existence away? I am beginning to be so afraid of all the thoughts that go through my mind as I notice every spirit candle starts to burn out along this pathway.

The air becomes cold and the thick mist that surrounds Barbara and the Witch starts to move closer to us along with the darkness. I feel the Entities' energy becoming stronger as they begin to move a little closer behind the cold thick mist coming from within the darkness. With every small movement, a spirit candle burns out behind them. Barbara follows close behind the mist which carries a dark energy that fills the air along with a rotted moldy stench that weakens my existence from the world I am trying to return to. Every emotion going through my mind at this moment becomes intense bringing so much anxiety from not wanting to face what is about to happen. The fiery ball held by the Dark Witch is the only light moving through the pathway. The Witch hovers like a reflection next to Barbara who is held back by Aunt Vera's presence, although Barbara is still making her way toward us.

I have had so many fears inside this nightmare, but my biggest fear comes from becoming trapped forever in a place filled with endless pathways leading to nothing. The essence of time does not seem to exist here. Time has stopped while being trapped inside this pathway. The darkness inside this dreadful place has become the eternity that allows no one to find any peace. I can only imagine the darkness keeping me from closing my eyes to dream again. A dream must have light to guide every thought, emotion, and memory to be kept inside my head, thus becoming a window to the outside world. Without the light to see out, only the darkness becomes an endless pathway leading into nothing, but the darkness filled with the shadow-like figures that stay hidden. I can only imagine without dreams I would be lost, never having a chance to look forward to what lies ahead for me. Becoming nonexistent to all those around me, only leaving behind the pain that I must face now with the images that have come and gone on this poorly lit path.   As I bring myself to face what would become the end to my existence, I turn to the Spirit who has been by my side all this time. Again, I ask her, "If you leave, I will no longer be protected from Barbara or the Dark Figures who wait to drag me away into their world."

Aunt Vera's spirit starts to back away from me while she smiles, reaching out to me with both of her hands. She says, "I have waited for you and now you will be alone to finish what you were brought here to do."

"Wait . . . Please . . . Please don't go."

The Spirit kneels to the ground as her white gown lays flat around her. The Spirit looks down toward the ground becoming this wavy, twisting bright image becoming too unbearable to watch. I knew she was starting to shape-shift back to the White Owl. I desperately started rubbing my eyes to keep my vision clear to watch out for the Dark Entities. I started to panic as I tried to focus on the things around me. The image of my Aunt Vera turns into a translucent white light far too bright to watch. Suddenly these white wings appear extending out of the bright light across the path. The bright light starts to fade, and the White Owl starts to appear. The spirit of my aunt is gone, as once again the White Owl stands on this path like a dream moving its large wings up and down in slow motion. I see Barbara and her Dark Entities moving toward me. I have no choice but to run into the dark walls along this path to get away.

As I get ready to run into the empty darkness, the White Owl grabs me by the back of my shirt and takes me into the air. The claws of the White Owl hold onto me while we disappear into the dark walls. I close my eyes, unaware of where we are going. I feel a sense of peace moving my legs around as if I were flying into a pitch-dark world. I am feeling relieved, yet unsure where or what the White Owl is going to do with me. I continue to keep my eyes closed even though I cannot help myself from wanting to look. I open my eyes while feeling my stomach start to hurt with the same sinking feeling when I become disembodied inside my bedroom. I am still unable to see anything through the pitch-black darkness all around us.

I push up against my stomach with both hands to ease the sinking feeling inside my stomach while praying to God to return to my family.

What seemed to feel like a long trip, we finally come to a stop. Feeling so scared and shaken, I slowly open my eyes to see where I am. I suddenly start to cry and laugh at the same moment. I cannot believe I am looking down at my bed. I quickly turn my head to look around my bedroom as my body is still lifting into the air near the ceiling. I do not see any sign of the White Owl. I suddenly feel too scared to shut my eyes, hoping not to be dragged into the dark pathway by Barbara ever again. I know I have to face my fear by shutting my eyes to end this nightmare. I slowly shut my eyes and feel myself starting to get the sinking feeling once more, so I know I am falling back into my bed.

I open my eyes, staring at the ceiling with a sense of peace and comfort going through my body instead of the overwhelming feeling of anxiety that stayed with me throughout this nightmare. There is still a part of me that still feels a little scared. A fear deep down inside me of something evil returning to finish what it tried to do to me inside its dark world. Does not matter anymore . . . I am inside my bedroom far away from those evil Dark Entities. Everything inside my bedroom seems so quiet. Only the sound of the rain hitting against the outside of my window. Nothing seems to have changed since I was dragged into the dark world. What seemed forever lost inside that pathway time did not pass. The time on the clock radio is ten o'clock—the exact time when I had fallen asleep after tossing and turning in bed for two hours. I continue to lie in bed feeling so confused about everything I experienced inside that cold dark pathway. I feel so many different emotions while staring around my bedroom. I begin to cry, feeling an overwhelming sadness. I am not sure why I feel this way. However, watching David disappear from my life was something that I did not want to experience again. I slowly got out of bed and walked over to my window to look outside at the old barn. I moved the curtain to the side and saw the rain coming down as I looked toward the barn. Still feeling unsure of what happened to me, I just stared at the old barn for a while. Suddenly I see something white moving from the opening of the barn near the roof. A reflection of two small lights glaring toward me. I knew it was the White Owl. I whispered, "Thank you, Aunt Vera . . . "

I suddenly heard a voice, "I will always be with you."

I looked around my bedroom to see if the spirit of my aunt was near me. Nothing . . . I was just hearing things. Suddenly I thought about what the spirit of my aunt had told me. I must confront what connects me to my nightmare. I must close the channel that allows Barbara to come and go as she pleases through the darkness. I needed to think about what my aunt's spirit was trying to tell me. How could I stop her from coming through this channel that connects the dark world she has created into my world? I did not want to be led back into the dark empty pathway. I knew I had to finish this. This nightmare was not over yet until I found a way to close the opening that would eventually come back to torment me.

I continued to watch the two small reflecting lights glaring back at me from the White Owl sitting just outside the opening of the barn. I started to yawn, so I slowly closed my curtain as I continued to look toward the barn. I walked back to my bed and covered myself up with my blanket. I covered my head up and closed my eyes.

I suddenly woke up to my father's voice calling out my name. I could hear my father calling me from the kitchen. "Robert . . . get yourself up so we can go find a Christmas tree."

Jumping out of bed, feeling so happy, I rubbed my eyes, staring out my window. The sunlight coming through the curtain looked so bright, something that I missed so much. Nothing made me happier than watching the sun come into my bedroom as I stood in front of my window. I stormed out of my bedroom and ran up to my father. I wrapped my arms around him to give him a hug. He said, "You ok, Robert?"

"I am now, Pop."

I jumped into my father's car, "Hey, Pop . . . do you miss David?"

My father looked at me and said, "Of course . . . every day I think about David."

"Do you think he is ok now?"

"Yes . . . why do you ask, Robert?"

"Just wondering . . . "

I looked out the window of the car as we drove into town, I turned back to look in the back seat behind my father and saw David's reflection in the window staring right at me with a smile. I sense David was happy and is now at peace. Just like the peace I saw with him when he was alive staring out the window of the car watching all the trees go by when we would take those long trips with our parents through the mountains. I saw the same smile when he stared out the window as we passed every tree along the road. I remember how excited David looked when Mom and Dad would stop along the road, and he would jump out of the car to look around while they would yell at him not to go too far. I would run behind David watching how free he felt, never thinking he would be running from something so dark that would haunt him during the night. I never knew, until now, how he had been suffering from all the nightmares. The sadness that still lingers inside me for not understanding what David was going through. I should have protected my brother. Because of this, I must end all this with Barbara for David.

We arrived home with the Christmas tree. Mom became so happy as she told us to put it next to the front window. She went into her bedroom to get a box filled with the large, colorful Christmas lights from the closet. I sat next to the tree on the floor waiting for her then asked if I could help. "Of course," she said, smiling.

I grabbed the Christmas lights out of the box and started untangling the strands of different color bulbs. Mom reached into another box and started taking out the ornaments. She then grabbed one of them and held on to it, staring at it for a while. I continued to hang the lights on the tree, and I noticed her still staring at what she was holding in her hand. I walked around the tree placing the lights and I noticed my mother now weeping. I said, "What's wrong?"

She looked at me and held her hand up to show me what she was holding. I smiled at her and asked if I could hang it on the tree. She wiped the tears from her face with the back of her hands and handed me the ornament. I stared at it for a bit, and Mom told me she remembered when David made it in 1978 at his school. Each time she takes the ornament out of the box I stay quiet even though she seems to forget that she tells me this every year. A picture of David's face glued to the ornament always reminds her how much she misses him. There is not a Christmas that goes by when I see Mom take the ornament out of the box that she doesn't start to cry as she holds it in her hand. The pain of her losing David never seems to go away as she holds onto something that is a constant reminder of that tragic night when she held him for the last time.

Even though a part of us was taken away, my parents try to make our time together enjoyable. Still feeling sad from watching Mom, I felt an overwhelming relief of being home with my family once again. I can only hope I will never have to face waking up in a place that almost took me away forever.

Once she and I had decorated the tree, Mom started to make her persimmon cookies like she does every Christmas. She asked me if I would go with her to see my Uncle Steve who lived alone in a small house just outside of town. My mother has not seen him for a couple of years. She decided to visit her brother and needed me to help her take a few things over to his house the next morning. Just knowing we had to go over to Uncle Steve's house made me nervous since he lived alone and did not talk to anyone.

My Uncle Steve served in Vietnam and would never talk about his time there. He lived alone, keeping himself secluded from all the family.

He had this stare as if he knew what you were thinking. Regardless of how I felt, I had no other choice but to go with Mom Even though I felt uncomfortable going over to see my uncle, nothing could be worse than what I had just gone through with my whole experience with the nightmare.

The night was starting to set in, and I knew I had to face another night home after returning from facing all the evil things that hid inside the darkness of that dreadful pathway. I just hoped that without closing the channel that my Aunt Vera had warned me about those Dark Entities would not come back for me during the night while I slept. I can still see those images inside my head of those evil monkey faces and Barbara, along with the Witch, watching me from the darkness along the pathway. I do not know what Barbara is going to do since I escaped from being trapped inside their world. I only know Barbara will find another way to get to me once more if I do not find a way to close the channel that connects me to her. Regardless of how worried I may seem from not completely closing the connection between me and Barbara, I had to shut my eyes and fall asleep. I closed the doors going into the bathroom and kitchen. I knelt on the floor next to my bed and thanked GOD for returning me to my parents. I finally got into my bed and covered myself up with my blanket. I looked around my bedroom and told myself, *"Just one more night and without any more nightmares."*

Even though I still was not looking forward to visiting my Uncle Steve at his place, I turned over on my side facing the clock radio while staring at the time and hoping for a peaceful night.

CHAPTER 19
FOREWARNING

I OPEN MY EYES STARING up into the darkness hearing a knocking going across my wall above my head. I started to become so terrified, I knew something was here. I covered my head with my blanket and felt scared of what I was about to face once again. I could hear a noise coming from inside my bedroom. A chanting of whispers all around me and a cold draft coming through my blanket. Somehow the Entities had made their way back to me. *"Oh, GOD . . . I don't want to go back."*

I begin to shake from being so scared along with the anxiety of seeing Barbara once again inside the pathway. "This cannot happen again . . . I don't want to go back."

I stayed still under my blanket, hoping all this would stop. I started to hear those familiar noises from outside my blanket; a low, screeching sound along with whispers that seemed to come from something wicked. The same screeching sound I would hear when a whistling breeze blows through the walnut trees at night when a storm starts to move in. Along with the screeching sound, I could hear the whispers manifesting all around me as I lay in bed horrified from not wanting to face Barbara once again. Suddenly, my blanket was pulled off me. I quickly grabbed my pillow and put it over me to protect myself. I open my eyes and see the dark figures around my bed. I yell for them to get away. Above me is the face of the Witch looking directly at me with its hideous face and large dark eyes. Its black smoke-like strands of hair hovering completely around my head as her face gets closer to my face. I close my eyes and start screaming. My bedroom light suddenly turns on and my mother said, "Why are you screaming?"

I quickly sat up and said, "I don't know."

Mom walked over to me and put my blanket over me as I lay back down. I was shaking and felt my clothes wet from sweating profusely from what seemed so real. I gasped with relief that I was just having a nightmare. Mom shut my light off and shut the door and said, "Get some rest, you'll have to be up early."

I turned back to my side, still shaken from that horrific nightmare. I forced myself to go back to sleep knowing that I needed to hurry to put an end to these nightmares.

I open my eyes and notice the sunlight coming in through my curtain. "*Oh . . . what a relief. Morning time.*"

I could hear my mom cooking in the kitchen, so I jumped out of bed and got ready. Once I got myself ready for my day with my mom, I went into the kitchen and sat down to eat my breakfast. She sat across from me next to my dad. I asked them how Aunt Vera had passed away. Pop said, "I thought I told you. She died from pneumonia and there was nothing the hospital could do to help her."

"Pop . . . did you talk to Uncle Joe when she was in the hospital?"

"Yes . . . why do you ask?"

"Did you ask Uncle Joe if anyone went to visit her other than the family?"

"No . . . but he did tell me about a night he woke up sleeping in the chair next to her hospital bed and about two-thirty in the morning hearing someone shutting the door going into their restroom. He thought it was Aunt Vera, watching a partially dark figure walk into the restroom. He felt this was strange since she was barely breathing on her own. He also noticed not seeing a light coming from under the bathroom door. He got up from the chair to see who went into the restroom, but nobody was there when he opened the door. Uncle Joe felt this was also strange that the door had shut by itself. He said the next night when he fell asleep after watching Aunt Vera, he gradually opened his eyes and he saw a man standing in the doorway going out into the hallway of the hospital. He got up from the chair to see what he wanted, and he suddenly walked away leaving by the elevator. He just thought this was strange."

"But . . . did Uncle Joe notice anything different before Aunt Vera got sick?"

"No . . . only telling me that he could not understand how she got pneumonia when she was perfectly fine the day before when she was going to call you guys on the phone about something important."

"What do you think she was going to tell us?"

"Not sure. Your Uncle Joe didn't know."

At that moment, I knew the spirit of Aunt Vera was right. Barbara found a way to kill Aunt Vera using the Entities she had created from her dark world. But . . . why did she want to kill my Aunt Vera? I held my fork in my hand thinking about why Barbara wanted to hurt Aunt Vera, so then I asked my dad, "Did Barbara know Aunt Vera?"

"Yes."

My mother stood up from her chair and said, "Let's get ready to go."

I got up from the kitchen table and walked out of the back door to leave with my mother, although I was still curious about what Aunt Vera was going to tell my dad.

After what seemed to feel like a long trip to my Uncle Steve's, we finally approached his house, which almost looked abandoned. My mother stopped next to his broken-down car sitting in the front yard. I slowly got out of the car and went to help Mom grab a bag from the trunk. I slowly walked up to the front door standing close to my mother. Uncle Steve answered the door and let us into his small house that smelled like old damp wood. It was dark inside. A small table and a couple of chairs were in the corner of his front room.

I stood next to my mother while she sat at the table talking to her brother for a while. During the whole time, he would look at me from the side of his eyes as if he knew something was wrong. I had this feeling he knew what I was going through with my nightmares. He stared at me closely, as if wanting to tell me something. After Mom told him about everything going on with the family, we finally got ready to leave. She was the first one to walk out the front door while I followed close behind her. Uncle Steve grabbed my arm just before I went out the door and said, "Take this and put it in your front pocket."

He took my hand and gave me a folded-up piece of paper. I did not look at it. I just stuck it in my front pocket like he told me to. I ran to the car and sat in the front seat, then saw Uncle Steve in the mirror on the door as he walked up to the car. He came over to where I was sitting and leaned toward the open window to say goodbye to me and my mother. He looked at me with a concerned look on his face while watching us drive away. I sat quietly all the way home, wondering what Uncle Steve had handed me at his house. I was afraid to look.

I felt sad for him, having no wife or kids. He seems so lonely not having anyone around. He is different than any of the other family members I know. I do not know what he went through when he served in the military, I only knew what my mother had told me about his time in Vietnam and how so many people were hurt or never made it home.

I will never know Uncle Steve very well, but the burden he seems to carry has made him distant from the rest of the family. He seems stuck in this lonely world with no one around but my mother who seldom visits him. The way he looked at me, he may have seen something inside me as he looked into my eyes, sensing the burden I have already started to carry. Whether this remains to be true, he knew something was wrong as he handed me that folded piece of paper I have yet to look at. I have been lost in my thoughts of being forced to carry the burden of what I have gone through. I need to continue to find a way to close the channel between me and Barbara's dark world before I find myself facing another horrible nightmare.

When we finally arrived home, I jumped out of the car and started heading to the walnut orchard. As I turned around to look toward the back porch, I noticed my father stopping my mother just before walking through the screen door. He started to talk to her as he held open the screen door while watching me walk off into the orchard. I continued to ignore what they were doing but then I heard Pop call to me. I turned around and both my parents were standing in the backyard waiting for me to join them. From what I could see, I knew this must be important. I approached my parents, feeling a little nervous. My father looked at me for a moment and then said someone from school called.

"When you return to school, you need to see the school psychologist," he said.

I felt nervous about returning to Dr. Scott's office, knowing he is not what he seems to be. A feeling of anxiety starts to go through my body. I know I am unable to refuse to see him. My parents will not believe me if I tell them what I saw inside my nightmare. I fear they will think I have gone crazy and send me away. Thinking about how I can avoid going back to see Dr. Scott, I ask my father who I will see when I return to school.

"A lady named Mrs. Cindy Paige."

"What happened to Dr. Scott? I thought I would have to go see him."

"He is in the hospital not doing so good," said my father. "At least that's what the person on the phone told me."

"Oh, okay"

My mother said, "Don't stay out too late. Get home before it gets dark."

I turned around to head back into the walnut orchard to make my way to the pond. I was relieved that I wouldn't be seeing Dr. Scott, although I was curious about what happened to him. Still feeling threatened by Barbara and her Dark Entities, I fear they may return anytime soon. I desperately needed to know what I must do to stop her from coming back into my life. I sat on the edge of the pond, throwing dirt rocks into the pond, thinking about everything I experienced inside that dark path. Suddenly, I remembered the paper my Uncle Steve gave me. I reached into my pocket and pulled out the folded piece of paper. I slowly began to open the paper which was folded very tight with something hard placed inside. As I held the paper in my hand, I tried to be careful not to drop what was given to me. Finally, after opening it all the way, I could not believe what I was looking at. I started to read what was on the paper while holding what was inside. The writing contained a warning. *"Look into the night and watch out of the corner of your eyes as the shadows move into the darkness. This is not your eyes playing tricks; this is what waits like vultures for any chance to drag you away into a world that consumes all that you have become. The window to the outside world that you live in now is the reality in which you must remain. If the night becomes your world, it is only a false perception of what is hidden inside. What is living inside the darkness must never escape through the channels which cross over into your world when you close your eyes at night. Remember . . . the reality in which you live comes from your dreams and remembered thoughts you hold onto. Unlike the reality placed upon you by the evil, which becomes unsettled through the nightmares leading you further into the darkness and becoming lost from all that you have ever known."*

Having little understanding of what the writing said, I was reminded of what I experienced through the nightmare of finding myself almost lost from never seeing my parents again. The words resembled every emotion of how I felt trying to understand "What was real" and "What was not" inside that dark pathway.

Although I am still uncertain about what I need to do, I wonder if this note in my hand could help me find the answer to what I am looking for. Could this be the key to closing the channel that leads the darkness into my world? I continue to sit on the edge of the pond staring out over the water, waiting and hoping I will know what I need to do next. I am suddenly thinking about how Barbara and Dr. Scott are siblings; about the man in the picture with them. The same man I saw in the image killing the lady and her son. How could all of this involve me and my family? Why would Barbara want to kill Aunt Vera? Nothing made any sense. I cannot talk to my parents about my nightmare. They would only think I was *really* crazy.

I stood up and placed everything in my pocket and made my way back to my house. Walking through the orchard, I started to smell a terrible rotted moldy stench. I had to stop to look around, remembering where I had smelled this before. Suddenly remembering where this smell came from, I began to get worried. *Oh, my God . . .* the smell came from those Entities inside the pathway. *Why have I started to smell it again?*

Quickly I ran home, almost falling to the ground as I kept looking around and feeling terrified. I ran until I reached the barn to catch my breath. I heard a noise coming from inside, but I was too scared to go in after all that I had gone through. Still feeling the fear, I forced myself to go inside. I went to the front of the barn and pushed open the large wooden door. I slowly squeezed my way in while smelling the dust coming from inside. Looking around, I stopped in the middle of the barn trying to see with the little light coming through the wooden shingles above me. I heard a cracking noise coming from somewhere inside. I looked up in the corner of the barn near the ceiling and saw two small glaring lights reflecting toward me. Suddenly the glaring lights moved into the light, and I saw the eyes of the White Owl. I was so happy to see it once again. Unlike before, the White Owl stood much smaller and didn't seem to look like an angel from the heavens to save me. This White Owl was real as it perched on the wooden beam watching me. I watched the White Owl for a moment and said, "What else do I need to do to close the channel that connects me to Barbara?"

The White Owl did not respond to what I was saying. I became frustrated and scared, not knowing what I needed to do. I knew the Dark Entities were coming back for me. I just could not close my eyes, knowing I would find myself inside the dark pathway again. Taken away by the Entities who were waiting for any chance of me having one of my disembodied nightmares and almost possessing my soul like before. Again, I spoke to the White Owl in a louder voice, "Why do you just watch me and not do anything to help me?"

Nothing. I gave up trying to get any answers from some old barn owl. Just as I put my head down, something fell to the ground. I was not sure what fell, but it seemed to have come from where the White Owl was sitting. I really could not see what it was. I slowly walked over to where it may have fallen while looking up toward the Owl staring directly at me. Keeping my eyes on the White Owl, I knelt on the ground, searching for anything noticeable with a little light coming in through the broken boards hanging off the sides of the barn. The dust started to make me sneeze as I moved my hands around the ground. Suddenly, I felt a piece of cloth. I picked it up and started to dust it off. I raised it up to the light, noticing it looked just like the white cloth that matched the spirit of my Aunt Vera's white gown.

This *cannot* be! I left it beside her back in the pathway. At that moment, I knew my Aunt Vera would be with me. I picked it up and put the cloth in my pocket, hoping I would be protected from anything evil trying to overtake me tonight. I looked at the White Owl, "Thank you."

I walked out of the barn and ran in through the back porch, closing the door quickly behind me. I could not believe I was now being followed by what I left behind on the path. I knew I could not allow Barbara to continue using her Black Magic to send over the Dark Entities to take over my soul. I had to stop Barbara. Hopefully, the cloth will keep me safe for now. I felt I needed to find Dr. Scott. He could be a part of what was going on with me. But, if Dr. Scott finds out that I know all about him, he may not be so nice. I fear he will do something bad to me or worse, have Barbara send her dark figures to come for me. I just need to put an end to Barbara, along with the nightmares she is using to haunt me.

My day finally ended, still I feared what I must face tonight. I open the curtain to my bedroom window and look around in the dark. I look toward the big barn and see those two glaring eyes coming from an opening near the roof. I close the curtain and crawl into bed, knowing my Aunt Vera's spirit is still with me. Unaware of what the night could bring, I take the cloth I found earlier out of my pocket and place it next to my head. I still feel a little nervous about waking up during the night and finding myself being confronted by something bad.

CHAPTER 20

FINAL REST

CLOSING MY EYES AS every thought starts to fade into the darkness surrounded by only the sounds of those who move throughout the night, leaving behind the whispers that become the night's breeze while passing through every tree as if another world has come to life.

This holds true . . . when I wake up during the night to look out from inside my bedroom window, I see the very essence of a world created by the darkness which seems to appear at certain moments when fear becomes a significant part of my life. It is the same world filled with all the profound dark figures along with the ugliness hidden within the night waiting to lure me into a place far from the only life I have ever known. For this reason, I am burdened by the curse that was once placed upon me and my brother, never allowing us to live a normal life. I see so many other kids around me live out their childhood without the nightmares that I have already endured at such a young age. Often, I wonder over and over if there will ever be a time when all my fears will disappear, along with the spirits which appear to me seeking out the peace they long for. With every hope of ending this nightmare, I think back to when everything started to happen to me and my brother. I thought about how everything changed after the night of our tragic loss. I still remember hearing those words coming from a dark figure who stood over my parents while they were in bed inside the one-bedroom house in town before moving out here in the country. Those same words that never seem to disappear from inside my head I still hear today, "I placed a curse on one of your kids to die in seven years."

Having no understanding of what any of it meant during that time, I would have never thought we would become affected by what was said. Not until that same night my brother's life was taken by the voice of that dark figure who I found out later to be Uncle Eddie. We were unaware of those years my brother and I were living with a curse that eventually began to affect David, causing his life to be taken.

After David's tragedy, the curse continued to follow me, causing me to go through the same things my brother had gone through. I never knew about the terrifying dark figures and the nightmares David had been experiencing from a curse placed upon us by Barbara. Unaware of the unsettling images David had to face just before his death. I was forced to watch my brother suffer, never realizing this curse was with us all along.

Now I understand what needs to be done. I believe the curse that was placed upon my brother and me by Barbara and Uncle Eddie can now be broken. Hopefully, I can finally end the curse when I close the channel which connects me to Barbara. I can live my life like the rest of the children in my school, never having to worry if I am going to find myself stuck in a dark path again with the possibility of never returning. Unfortunately, I have yet to close the world which waits just outside this house during the night. Still, I need to desperately finish what I have come back home to do—stop the curse.

I began to slowly shut my eyes as I felt myself becoming uncontrollably sleepy. The thoughts continued to linger as I whispered, "Stop the curse . . . stop the curse," finally falling to sleep.

Soon, I am awakened by a fear of the complete darkness inside my bedroom. It is so quiet with only the sounds of the rain just outside my window. I am looking up toward the ceiling unable to see anything. I only see spots coming from my eyes as my vision tries to adjust to what I'm looking at. Slowly getting out of bed, I see my nightlight plugged into the outlet near my bed. I turn on my nightlight and quickly jump back into bed.

It is 2:35 a.m. and I am reminded how much I hate to be in a place so dark. Not wanting to be in complete darkness ever again only brings back my time inside the dark pathway. I force myself to go back to sleep, but unfortunately I have this unnerving feeling of still knowing those Entities are hiding somewhere inside the darkness surrounding me. I cannot help but wonder if they are already here with me. The terrible stench that lingered earlier from inside the orchard makes me think they *have* come back. Again, the fear of what I went through on that dark path still sits in the back of my mind, making it difficult for me to close my eyes. I cannot get rid of the thought of what I would be facing if this nightmare continues.

I turn on my side to look at the time on my clock radio, and suddenly become terrified at seeing a little boy standing in front of my bedroom window with his head looking down toward the floor with something dripping from his head. So frightened, I cannot move; staring at him as he just stands there. Feeling overwhelmed with disbelief, I finally grab my blanket and cover my head. I told myself *"This is only a dream."* I was so shaken by what I saw I had to look again to see if I was only seeing something that was not *really* there. I slowly lowered my blanket from my face and saw a lady holding the little boy's hand, walking toward the bathroom. I was horrified by the image of the same murdered mother and her son I first saw inside the pathway. I watched them gradually disappear into the darkness. Quickly, I covered my head, feeling the anxiety of seeing the images now inside my bedroom. Everything I went through before has somehow followed me home. If the images I saw back inside the pathway are now showing up here with me, there is a possibility I will soon face the Dark Witch and those dark figures once again. I desperately need to find a way to stop all the evil things from the dark world I just left behind. I believe they will manifest into my world and continue to terrorize me until I end up like my brother David.

As I lie in bed, I am thinking how important tomorrow will be for me to find Dr. Scott and learn the truth behind him and Barbara. I am only left with the images and the nightmares, which tell me truly little about why I continue to be haunted by so many bad things. What has led Barbara to the point where she wants to inflict harm on my family and intentionally remove me from my parents like she did with my brother? I am hoping Dr. Scott will tell me what I need to know to put an end to all of this.

I just remembered the white cloth I placed next to my head. I sat up in bed, looking around for the cloth. Now really worried, I got out of bed and threw my blankets on the floor. I did not see the cloth anywhere lying on my bed. Picking up my blanket, I knelt on the floor, looked underneath my bed, and found nothing. I sat up on the edge of my bed and looked over to where the little boy and his mother were standing, and there it was, lying on the floor near my bedroom window. I walked over to pick it up. I thought to myself, *how did the white cloth end up over there?* Lying down back in bed, I felt safe now knowing I had the cloth back with me. Still, I was confused about how the cloth ended up across the room. Could this be another sign to let me know the little boy's spirit is still searching for peace? Nevertheless, I have it now and I can finally get to sleep. The thought of the little boy somehow being connected to me and my brother remains. Hopefully, I can find more answers tomorrow. I covered my head with my blanket and put my hands over my ears, finally falling back to sleep. I was still shaken about what I just experienced but now I was just plain exhausted.

As soon as I closed my eyes, I put my hands over my face to block the sunlight coming into my bedroom. I slowly got out of bed, placing the white cloth under my pillow next to the small Bible. I went into the kitchen where I heard my mother making breakfast. I sat on the chair at the kitchen table and stared at my mother for a while. Finally, I asked, "Do you know Uncle Eddie's wife, Barbara, very well?"

"Not very well," she said. "Barbara didn't like anyone. She always seemed so angry when I did see her with Uncle Eddie before you were born."

"Why do you think Barbara was so mean?"

"Well . . . Barbara always seemed so withdrawn from everyone. She would try to avoid coming out of her house. She only left her house at night from what I heard from people that have known her since she was very young. Other people say her father was abusive toward her. I also heard she had a brother who died suddenly."

"Mom . . . are you sure Barbara's brother isn't still alive?"

"As far as I know, he died."

"Do you know his name?"

"I think his name was Edward . . . not sure what his last name was."

"Do you think Barbara was mad about what happened to her brother?"

"I don't know."

"How old was Edward when he died?"

"I think he was about your age."

I thought it was strange that Barbara had a brother named Edward who died. Who is the little boy next to the little girl in the picture hanging up in Dr. Scott's office? I thought the little boy in the picture was Dr. Edwind Scott and the little girl was Barbara. If that is not Dr. Scott, how does he know the man and the two kids in that picture?

Mom finally said, "Robert, go get ready. I have to go to town to pick up a few things."

I quickly left the table and went to my bedroom to change. I put on my pants that were hanging in the closet while sticking my hands in the front pocket. I still had the paper Uncle Steve had given me, so I left it there and grabbed the white cloth from under my pillow. I ran out through the back porch and got in the car. I sat in the front seat looking out the window at the old barn as we drove out of our driveway. I wondered where the White Owl goes during the day and if it returns to a dark world to wait for the night to set in, only to come back to watch over me. I wondered if my Aunt Vera's soul was trapped inside the White Owl, having already seen her shape-shift inside the pathway. I wonder if she feels at peace looking out from the White Owl's eyes and flying free from one world to another. Or does she want to be released from being trapped within the White Owl, desiring the peace that every soul longs for? Either way, I feel she must be lonely, unable to be with her family ever again.

Just as my mother and I were pulling up to the road leaving our house, I saw a car drive by. I saw a girl about my age sitting in the back seat. I just stared at her while she stared back at me as the car drove right past us. I did not really think too much about seeing anyone other than a tractor or farmer driving down this road. I just stared at the car, feeling dazed out. My mother looked over at me and asked, "You okay? . . . you have this faraway look in your eyes."

"I'm okay," I said.

We drove on into town, pulling up to a store across the street from the hospital—the only hospital we had inside our small town. I asked my mother if I could go to the hospital after we got what we came for from the store.

"Why? Are you feeling sick?"

"No . . . I want to see if Dr. Scott is still in the hospital."

"Ok, I can take you as soon as we are done here." Mom looked at me with a look of concern while nodding her head.

I walked through the store with my mother, trying to prepare myself to see Dr. Scott, unaware of what type of condition he might be in. Feeling so nervous, I could not think about anything else when she asked me about what I would like to eat for dinner. I just could not stop thinking about what I wanted to say to Dr. Scott. Nothing could prepare me for what I was about to do when I went to the hospital. All I could think about was not wanting to face any more of the evil conceived by such a mean person, who had already made my life so terrible. I could only hope for the truth behind all the bad things that I had to face since my brother's death.

As I stood inside the store I wondered what Mom would think about everything that I have seen inside the nightmares and the dark place I had just come back from. All the fears I have and all the thoughts that go through my mind would become overwhelming for my parents to deal with—especially Mom, having to deal with the loss of one of her children. She would have to face the pain all over again, remembering what she had gone through while trying to be there for me. I imagine nothing could be more painful than to watch her become upset again at seeing something else happening to another one of her children. I must face Dr. Scott alone and hope he can find it in his heart to help me.

My mother and I finally left the store and she drove me across the street to the hospital. She got out of the car with me. I took a deep breath as we approached the lady at the front desk and Mom asked, "Is Dr. Edwind Scott in this hospital?"

"Yes, he is. Can I ask who is here to see him?"

"My son, Robert De Le Cruz."

The desk clerk told my mom she had to come with me. Mom led me to the elevator. We reached the floor and at the room where Dr. Scott was, she said, "I will wait for you outside the door . . . ok?"

"Ok."

I walked into the room and saw this man lying down in the long bed. The smell seemed very strange, like the smell of iodine. I walked up to his bedside as he seemed so peaceful, sleeping there. He gradually opened his eyes and turned to look at me.

"Robert . . . how *are* you . . . ?"

"I'm fine, Dr. Scott." I just stared at him with so many thoughts going through my head.

Dr. Scott smiled at me and said, "Thank you for stopping by to see me . . . Robert."

He knew why I was there. He looked at me with a tear running down his cheek and said, "Do you remember when I told you to never hold onto stuff too long. You will find yourself surrounded by really bad things that will keep you from being happy?"

"Yes . . . I remember, Dr. Scott."

"Well . . . when I told you about the story of the mother and her son who were killed in their backyard. I did not tell you everything that happened in the story. I was young during that time. I had to go live with my uncle and my two cousins named Eddie and his little sister named Barbara in their small house in town. My parents were killed in an automobile accident while they were drinking. I was left all alone at home while waiting for them to return. A couple of days went by, and my parents never came back. I had to walk to my uncle's home to stay with him and his two kids. I learned about the accident later from my uncle who also told me I would have to live with them. I never felt so alone, even though I was with family.

"I started to see things inside my uncle's house—things that were not particularly good. He would tell me to get to bed and I could hear noises coming from downstairs. I heard screaming and doors slamming every night. I would get up early and Eddie and Barbara would be sitting in the kitchen quietly eating. I walked to school with them, but they would not tell me anything and seemed very afraid of their father. Later, Eddie and I were out in the front yard playing catch and his father called him into the house to do something he was supposed to have done in the morning. I stood outside waiting for Eddie to finish playing ball with him. Only his father came out and I could hear the panic in his voice. He said, 'Eddie is dead. I must have hit him too hard.'

"I just stared at my uncle as he sat there talking to himself. He went back inside and carried Eddie outside to the backyard and laid him on the ground. This was deemed an accident. My uncle continued to abuse Barbara and it was not much later that I learned his wife was found dead outside when his kids were small. This too was also deemed an accident. My uncle has passed away and he was never charged with the murder of his wife and son. Barbara became angry like her father, withdrawn from everyone around her. She studied Black Magic, using it against anyone who tried to go against her. Waiting for any chance to hurt someone she found threatening.

"Barbara did have a child long ago. Unfortunately, the child was run over by a car. Barbara always suspected the driver of the car to be your father. He was there when it happened, leading her to believe that he was the one who did it. Barbara became incredibly angry, blaming your father by cursing his children to die in seven years, the same age her son was when he was killed."

"Did my father kill Barbara's son?"

"That is a question to ask your father. I had no choice but to be by Barbara's side. Turning away from what she was doing to you and your family, I became a school psychologist to help children. Unfortunately, Barbara used me to continue to make your father pay for what he did."

Dr. Scott turned away from me with tears falling on both sides of his face. He slowly turned to look at me for a moment and asked me to hold out my hand. It was the locket like the one he told me about the first time he told me this story back at his office. I opened the locket and saw the mother and the little boy I had seen inside the image back on the dark path. The same spirit of the murdered boy who appeared next to Dr. Scott inside the dark and cold pathway.

I knew what I needed to do to end all of this. I took out of my pocket what my Uncle Steve gave me. I placed it in Dr. Scott's hand and helped him by squeezing it with the little strength he had. He turned away from me and looked toward the ceiling. I watched the air expel from his mouth while the alarms went off from his breathing machine. I knew he was gone. Everyone from the hospital came running into the room trying to revive him. My mother put her arm over my shoulders and told me it was time for us to leave. I looked at my mother and said, "I think everything will be okay now."

I looked back into the room from the hallway feeling sad for Dr. Scott. Feeling a sense of closure, I finally felt the peace. Free from the curse that has been with me from the very beginning of my life. Hearing the pain from his voice, I knew Dr. Scott wanted to find peace within himself, before letting out his last breath. Taking along the darkness which had kept him imprisoned by the same evil. Connecting us through the nightmares forced onto to us by the same person who watches and waits, only to feed off our fears and vulnerability. I knew I had to give Dr. Scott something that would finally close the channel between me and Barbara for now. A cross . . . something Uncle Steve handed to me along with the forewarning written down on a piece of paper. A cross I knew all too well. The same cross Uncle Steve picked up from his floor after David and our mother had paid him a visit. Never having the chance to give the cross back to David due to his passing, he held onto it until he gave the cross to me. I felt giving it to Dr. Scott would allow him to know the life he lived revolved around the darkness that placed so much pain within my family.

I sat quietly in the front seat of the car heading back home while thinking about how I felt watching Dr. Scott become just another transient, leaving the only life he knew, entering another unknown world forever. Maybe . . . Dr. Scott handing me the locket could help him put an end to what he was also being haunted by, finally finding the peace he never found when he was alive. Having the locket makes me wonder what I need to do with it.

Arriving back to our house, Mom and I did not say anything to Pop about what happened today. I never asked him about what Dr. Scott told me about Barbara blaming my father for her son's death. I just wanted to live my life free from evil. I desperately wanted all of this to go away, along with the nightmares to keep me from being reminded of Barbara's presence.

CHAPTER 21
CLOSURE

AFTER FEELING A SENSE OF peace sitting in my bed, I was ready to fall asleep while feeling so tired and hoping for a full night's rest as I looked under my pillow to make sure the white cloth was still there.

I lay down staring at the ceiling, feeling as if all the bad things I experienced were finally gone. Hoping the connection I had with Barbara and the world she created would be gone from my life forever. I turned to my side to look at my clock radio wondering what David is doing right now in the world he is in. Having given him the cross I found inside the wooden box back inside the pathway, I knew David was now at peace—especially knowing it belongs to him. I thought about how Uncle Steve had the same cross he found on the floor years before and handed it to me when I gave David's spirit the same cross back inside the pathway. The same cross I found inside the old record player, knowing it belonged to him. I feel as if David had spiritually attached himself to the cross that had manifested into the dark world that I barely escaped from. Being inside such a place made it possible for me to hand it over to him, while the physical form of the cross was meant for me to give to Dr. Scott in hopes of ending all of this.

Still skeptical about what might have followed me from the dark pathway and might still be lurking in the dark, I felt a little cautious closing my eyes. Placing my blanket over my head still lying on my side, I could feel myself finally falling asleep. No sooner had I closed my eyes than I heard a strange noise coming from inside my bedroom. I suddenly opened my eyes, unable to bring myself to look to see what it was. I stayed unmoving under my blanket, hoping the noise I heard was from being half-asleep. Then I heard the noise again, a creaking sound near my window. I slowly stuck my hand under my pillow to feel the white cloth. I grabbed it and closed my eyes, trying to force myself to go back to sleep. I knew there was something inside my bedroom.

I lowered my blanket from my eyes and barely looked over the edge. I saw the spirit of the murdered little boy and his mother near my window. My body froze! Something inside told me to get the locket. Remembering the locket was still in my front pocket, I took it out and I slowly started to wrap it up in the white cloth. I looked around in the dark, making sure I did not see anything else. I cautiously started to walk toward the two spirits. I watched them standing near the window as my curtain moved behind them. I got close enough to place the locket on the floor near them. The spirit of the little boy knelt near the locket, staring at it for a while. The spirit of the boy stood up and grabbed his mother's hand and they started walking toward my bathroom door, disappearing into the dark.

At that moment, it was all over. The circle had finally been closed and the channel that bridges all the suffering I had to face was now completely shut.

I can finally be at peace and live my life like the other kids I go to school with. Without the nightmares each night and the dark figures haunting me, I no longer feel Barbara's energy here with me. I can only hope I have seen the last of Barbara's evil intentions of wanting to make my father pay for something that he did not do.

I sit up in my bed staring toward my window where the mother and the little boy were standing. I could still feel my chest pounding while my fear started to slowly go away. I found it difficult to go back to sleep after watching the images appear to me with a sad look coming across their face. I do not know if they finally found what they came here for. They are now free from the dark pathway just like my brother—the same dark pathway that trapped my soul and was not allowing me to return to my world. The pathway Barbara used to channel our souls into her evil world, only failing to do so by not having enough dark energy to pull us in.

This dark pathway sits somewhere in another world, waiting for a soul to be trapped until its purpose is found. Unaware of what has happened, the soul waits for someone or something to help guide them to where they must go. I do not know if I was the person who was supposed to help those souls inside the pathway to find their way back. I only know I have found *my* purpose. I am the exception, returning to my family. The other souls will never have a chance to return to their family. Although I believe the souls that become transients after their life has ended will not be the end to their existence; only a beginning to a new life. Whether trapped inside a dark pathway or moving on to another world, it seems as if our soul carries us until returning to another life with the hope of meeting a new family or the ones we have left behind from another time.

This I why I believe my life will never end. There will be a return to a life created by memories and emotions all over again; strengthening the spirit, which becomes a continuation of our existence. I now know my purpose is to live on and raise my family.

I slowly get up from bed to look out the window to see if the owl is watching our house. I can see two small reflections coming from the opening near the roof. I have finally felt peace, knowing I am not alone. I look around in the dark just before closing my curtain and suddenly notice a dark figure on the side of the barn, partially hidden. Watching the figure closely, I am convinced it is just a shadow coming from a tree. But then as I start to close my curtain, I see the dark figure move away from the barn. Fright and anxiety once again become overwhelming and I get a severe pain in my stomach. I quickly close my curtain. I cannot believe what I just saw. The dark figure was standing in front of the barn. It looks like a black gown waving along with the pitch-black strands moving with the night's breeze. Confused, I walk slowly over to my bed. I gasp for air with an unsettling feeling while getting back into bed. I am staring into the darkness, looking up toward the ceiling.

THE END

ABOUT THE AUTHOR

ALBERT BAIZ GARCIA

This is the second book in the *Rivulet of Darkness* series written by author Albert Baiz Garcia. A native of Hanford, California, where he still lives and works today, Garcia studied English Literature and Writing at West Hills College. A devoted father and grandfather, Garcia believes his creative imagination and ongoing efforts to perfect his writing skills will be the most important legacy he can leave for the enjoyment of his family for generations to come. The third and final book of the series, *The Faceless Image*, will be published later this year.

AVAILABLE AT

 AMAZON

 BARNES & NOBLE

 (559) 836-4070

 albertbgarcia559@yahoo.com

 www.albertbgarcia.com